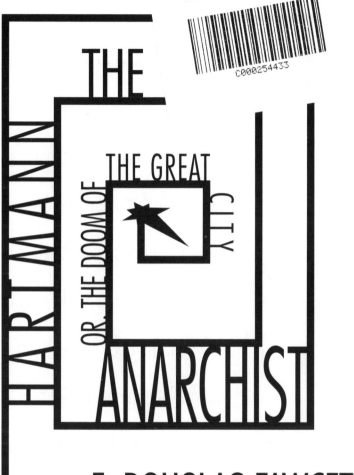

THE

THE GREAT

HARTMANN

OR, THE DOOM OF

CITY

ANARCHIST

E. DOUGLAS FAWCETT

contents

introduction

If you thought Ursula Le Guin was the best of anarchist science fiction wait till you read 'Hartmann the Anarchist: or The Doom of the Great City'.

Rudolph Hartmann is one hell of a guy. It was just his misfortune to be born ahead of his time. If in the summer of 2009 his airship the 'Attila' had appeared over London and blasted parliament to smithereens before moving off to annihilate the bankers in the city, he would have been a national hero. Even more so if he'd have taken a few of the Met G20 police officers out en route. The country would have been at his feet. His analysis of the reasons to bomb the City of London show his prescient awareness of the evils of globalisation years before anyone else:

'His aim was to pierce the ventricles of the heart of civilisation, that blood that pumps the blood of capital everywhere, through the arteries of Russia, of Australia, Of India, through the capillaries of the fur companies of North America, mining enterprises in Ecuador and the trading steamers of African rivers'

Echoing the old masthead of Green Anarchist, Hartmann wants nothing less than the 'destruction of civilisation' – achieved by pouring leaden death from the skies. No reformist, he.

But Hartmann has secret helpers on the ground – Nechaev style conspirators numbering 12,000 in London alone. They have already blown up the Home secretary's house (Angry Brigade) and burned down half of rich Kensington.

There are of course...ahem...a few minor quibbles about Hartmann's class analysis... referring to the working class as 'the swinish multitude' he's not particular if they also perish as they 'have long colluded with the system'. But this is to quibble in the face of genius... and anyway, Hartmann is justifiably miffed with them for failing to rise up during his earlier assassination attempt on the Crown Prince on Westminster Bridge. As with Emile Henri and Ravachol – there are no innocents for Rudolph Hartmann. I take it that Hartman's contempt for 'the swinish multitude' is in fact nothing more than a modish rejection of late Victorian consumerism!

So just relax and enjoy parliament and the bankers in the City of London being annihilated by good old-fashioned bomb-wielding anarchists.

Hartmann, written by E. Douglas Fawcett when he was only 17 years old, was Captain Nemo and Robur the Conqueror taken one stage further than Verne anticipated. First published in 1892 and not reprinted in full for over 100 years this is a long lost must-read anarchist classic. It spawned many others the best of which is Richard Chetwynd's 'Angel of the Revolution' and created a whole genre of crazed anarchist airship commanders with which to terrify the readers. Many of these commanders were like Rudolph Hartmann 'members of the professional classes gone bad' leading even to what must be one of the most obscure doctoral theses of all time... 'Class treachery in airship commanders in late Victorian fiction' by Haza Shpayer-Makov. Many of these can be viewed at the excellent 'Anarchism in Science Fiction' website. Unfortunately, what cannot be viewed, is the 15 minute sci-film made by William Booth in 1911 'The Aerial Anarchists' based on Hartmann and showing the bombing of St. Pauls. No footage has survived.

For a 17 year old public school boy E. Douglas Fawcett shows an amazing awareness of splits in the socialist movements and himself led a remarkable life. He was a Theosophist, climbed the Matterhorn aged 66, was an accomplished skier and motorcycle racer, and became a pilot when he was 84. His younger brother was the famed lost explorer Percy Fawcett who vanished in the Amazon jungle in 1925 looking for the 'lost City of Z'. Whether he ever found it we do not know but expeditions to 'Find Fawcett' were mounted for decades afterwards and sightings reported well into the 1960s.

The original illustrations in the book were by Fred Janes – a commercial artist with a penchant for death raining airships. He went on to found the 'Janes Fighting Ships' reference series which exists till this day. I think Stanley Donwood has succeeded in capturing the spirit of these originals in a unique form.

'Hartmann' has for decades only been available at a prohibitive price in the E.Arnold first edition published in 1892 or in the 'Forgotten Fantasy' series in 1971– which went belly up before they could publish the second half – or in some soulless print on demand version with no feel for the original. So here it is at last – a lost anarchist classic.

Comrades – Keep watching the skies!

Ian Bone, 2009

First published 1892 by E Arnold
This edition published 2009 by Bone

ISBN: 9781906477288

Bone is an imprint of Tangent Books
Unit 5.16 Paintworks
Arnos Vale
Bristol
BS4 3EH

0117 972 0645

www.tangentbooks.co.uk
email: richard@tangentbook.co.uk

Publisher: Ian Bone
Images: Stanley Donwood
Design: Nick Law

Bone are interested in publishing radical
biographies/autobiographies both contemporary
and historical. If you've got an idea try it out on us.
www.ianbone.wordpress.com
localnews4us@yahoo.co.uk

1. Dark Hints

All things considered, I rate October 10th, 1920, as the most momentous day of my life. Why it should be so styled is not at once apparent. My career has not been unromantic; during many years I have rambled over the globe, courting danger wherever interest led me. More than once I have tripped near the cave where Death lies in ambush. I am now an old man, but my memory is green and vigorous. I can look back calmly on the varied spectacle of life and weigh each event impartially in the balance. And thus looking, I refer my most fateful experience to an hour during an afternoon conversation in my dull, dingy, severe-looking quarters in Bayswater.

From romance to the commonplace is seldom a long trudge. On this occasion a quite commonplace letter determined my destiny. There was nothing of any gravity in the letter itself. It was a mere invitation to meet some friends. Most people would stare vacantly were I to show it to them. They would stare still more vacantly were I to say that it enabled me to write this terrible story. Bear in mind, however, that a lever, insignificant in itself, switches an express train off one track on to another. In a like manner a very insignificant letter switched me off from the tracks of an ordinary work-a-day mortal into those of the companion and biographer of a Nero.

Some two years before the time of which I write I had returned to London, having completed a series of adventurous travels in Africa and South-West Asia. My foregoing career is easily briefed. Left an orphan of very tender years, I had grown up under the ægis of a bachelor uncle, one of those singularly good-hearted men who rescue humanity from the cynics. He had always treated me as his own son, had given me the advantages of a sterling education, and had finally crowned his benevolence by adopting me as his heir. An inveterate politician, he had early initiated me into the mysteries of his cult, and it is probably to his guidance that I owed much of my later enthusiasm for reform.

As a youngster of twenty-three I could not, however, be expected to abandon myself to blue-books and statistics, and was indeed much more intent on amusement than anything else. Among my chief passions was that of travel, a pursuit which gratified both the acquired interests of culture and the natural lust of adventure. Of the raptures of the rambler I accordingly drank my fill, forwarding, in dutiful fashion, long accounts of my tours to my indulgent relative. Altogether I spent three or four years harvesting rich experience in this manner. I was preparing for a journey through Syria when I received a telegram from my uncle's doctor urging me immediately to return. Being then at Alexandria I made all haste to comply with it, only, however, to discover the appeal too well grounded, and the goal of my journey a death-bed. I mourned for my uncle's loss sincerely, and my natural regrets were sharpened when his will was read. With the exception of a few insignificant bequests, he had transferred his entire property to me.

The period of mourning over, I was free to indulge my whims to the utmost, and might well have been regarded as full of schemes for a life of wild adventure. Delay, however, had created novel interests; some papers I had published had been warmly welcomed by critics; and a new world – the literary and political – spread itself out seductively before me. Further, I had by this time seen "many cities and men," and the hydra-headed problem of civilization began to appeal to me with commanding interest. The teachings also of my uncle had duly yielded their harvest, and ere long I threw myself into politics with the same zeal which had carried me through the African forests, and over the dreary burning sands of Araby. I became, first a radical of my uncle's school, then a labour advocate and socialist, and lastly had aspired to the eminence of parliamentary candidate for Stepney. A word on the political situation.

Things had been looking very black in the closing years of the last century, but the pessimists of that epoch were the optimists of ours. London even in the old days was a bloated, unwieldy city, an abode of smoke and dreariness startled from time to time by the angry murmurs of labour. In 1920 the Colossus of cities held nigh six million souls, and the social problems of the past were intensified. The circle of competence was wider, but beyond it stretched a restless and dreaded democracy. Commerce had received a sharp check after the late Continental wars, and the depression was severely felt. That bad times were coming was the settled conviction of the middle classes, and to this belief was due the Coalition Government that held sway during the year in which my story opens. In many quarters a severe reaction had set in against Liberalism, and a stronger executive and repressive laws were urgently clamoured for. At the opposite extreme flew the red flag, and a social revolution was eagerly mooted.

I myself, though a socialist, was averse to

barricades. 'Not revolution, but evolution' was the watchword of my section. Dumont has said that 'the only period when one can undertake great legislative reforms is that in which the public passions are calm and in which the Government enjoys the greatest stability.' Of the importance of this truth I was firmly convinced. What was socialism? The nationalization of land and capital, of the means of production and distribution, in the interests of a vast industrial army. And how were the details of this vast change to be grappled with amid the throes of revolution? How deliberate with streets slippery with blood, the vilest passions unchained, stores, factories, and workshops wrecked, and perhaps a starving populace to conciliate? What man or convention could beat out a workable constitution in the turmoil? What guarantee had we against a reaction and a military saviour? By all means, I argued, have a revolution if a revolution is both a necessary and safe prelude of reform. But was it really necessary or even safe?

Feeling ran high in this dispute. Many a time was I attacked for my 'lukewarmness' of conviction by socialists, but never did I hear my objections fairly met. Though on good terms with the advanced party as a whole, I was opposed at Stepney by an extremist as well as by the sitting Conservative member. My chances of election were poor, but victorious or not I meant to battle vigorously for principle. To a certain extent my perseverance bore good fruit. During the last month I had been honoured with the representation of an important body at a forthcoming Paris Convention, and was in fact on the eve of starting on my journey. There was no immediate call for departure, but the prospect of a pleasant holiday in France proved overwhelmingly seductive. The Socialist Congress was fixed for October 20th, and I proposed to enjoy the interval in true sybaritic fashion. Perhaps my eagerness to start was not unconnected with a tenderer subject than either rambling or politics. Happily or unhappily, however, these dispositions were about to receive short shrift.

It was a raw dismal afternoon, the grim fog-robed buildings, the dripping vehicles, and the dusky pedestrians below reminding one forcibly of the 'City of Dreadful Night.' Memories of Schopenhauer and Thomson floated slowly across my mind, and the gathering shadows around seemed fraught with a gentle melancholy. Having some two hours before me, I drew my chair to the window and abandoned myself wholly to thought. What my meditations were matters very little, but I remember being vigorously recalled to reality by a smart blow on the shoulder.

"No, Stanley, my boy, it's no use – she won't look your way."

I looked up with a laugh. A stalwart individual with a thick black beard and singularly resolute face had broken upon my solitude.

This worthy, whose acquaintance we shall improve hereafter, was no other than John Burnett, journalist and agitator, a man of the most advanced revolutionary opinions, in fact an apostle of what is generally known as anarchical communism. No law, no force, reference of all social energies to voluntary association of individuals, were his substitutes for the all-regulating executive of the socialists. He made no secret of his intentions – he meant to wage war in every effective mode, violent or otherwise, against the existing social system. Though strongly opposed to the theories, I was not a little attached to the theorist. He talked loudly, but, so far as I knew, his hands had never been stained with any actual crime. Further, he was most sincere, resolute, and unflinching – he had, moreover, once saved me from drowning at great risk to himself, and, like so many other persons of strong character, had contracted a warm affection for his debtor.

That his visits to me were always welcome I cannot indeed say. Many rumours of revolutions and risings were in the air, and some terrible anarchist outrages reported from Berlin had made the authorities unusually wary. Burnett, in consequence, was a marked man, and his friends and acquaintances shone with a borrowed glory. Moderate as were my own views, they might conceivably be a blind, and this possibility had of late been officially recognized. It was wonderful what a visiting list I had, and still more wonderful that my callers so often chose hours when I was out. However, as they found that I was guiltless of harbouring explosives and had no correspondence worth noting, their attentions were slowly becoming infrequent. Burnett, too, had been holding aloof of late, indeed I had not been treated to his propaganda for some weeks. To what was the honour of this unexpected visit due? "Off to Paris, I hear," he continued. "Well, I thought I might do worse than look in. I have something to tell you too."

"My dear fellow," I cried, "you choose your time oddly. I must leave this place in a trice. Meanwhile, however, tell me where you've been of late, and what this latest wrinkle is."

"I? Well, out of London. If you had not been rushing off at short notice I might have spoken more to the point. You can't stay a couple of days longer, can you? Say yes, and I will engage to open your eyes a bit."

"No, I fear I can't: the Congress is not till the 20th, but meantime I want rest. I am positively done up.

Time enough, however, later on."

Burnett laughed. "It is worthwhile sometimes to take time by the forelock. Look here, I am bound hand and foot at present, but this I will say, your congresses and your socialism – evolutionary, revolutionary, or what not – are played out."

"I think I have heard that remark before," I somewhat coldly rejoined; "still, say what you like, you will find that we hold the reins. I won't say anything more of the practicability of anarchism, we have talked the matter over ad nauseam. But this I will say. Compared with us you are a handful of people, politically speaking of no account, and perhaps on the whole best left to the attention of the police. Forgive my bluntness, but to my mind, your crusade, when not absurd, appears only criminal."

"As you like," said Burnett doggedly; "the world has had enough barking – the time for biting has come. Restrain your eloquence for a season, and I'll promise you a wonderful change of convictions."

"What, have your Continental friends more wrecking in hand? What idiocy is this wretched campaign! It converts no one, strengthens the hands of the reactionaries, and, what is more, destroys useful capital. Why, I say, injure society thus aimlessly?"

"Curse society!" – and a heavy fist struck my writing-table – "I detest both society as it is and society as you hope it will be. Today the capitalist wolves and a slavish multitude; tomorrow a corrupt officialism and the same slavish multitude, only with new masters. But about our numbers, my friend, you think that we must be politically impotent because we are relatively so few. We count only our thousands where you tot up your millions of supporters. Obviously we could hardly venture to beard you after the established orthodox fashion. But suppose, suppose, I say, our people had some incalculable force behind them. Suppose, for instance, that the leaders of these few thousands came to possess some novel invention – something that – that made them virtual dictators to their kind" – and looking very hard at me he seemed to await my answer with interest.

"Suppositions of this sort are best kept for novels. Besides, I see no scope even for such an invention – it is part of the furniture of Utopia. But, stay! was not this invention the dream of that saintly dynamiter Hartmann also? Hartmann! Now there's a typical case of genius wasted on anarchy. A pretty story is that of your last martyr – tries to blow up a prince and destroys an arch and an applewoman. For the life of me I can't see light here!"

"All men bungle sometimes," growled the revolutionist, ignoring the first part of my reply; "Hartmann with the rest – ten years ago was it?

Ah! he was young then. But mark me, my friend, don't call people martyrs prematurely. You think Hartmann went down with that vessel – permit me to express a doubt."

"Well," I responded, "it matters little to me anyhow, but, anarchy apart, how that poor old mother of his would relish a glimpse of him, if what you hint at is true!"

He nodded, and involuntarily my thoughts ran back to the days of 1910, when my uncle read me, then a mere boy, the account of Hartmann's outrage.

As Hartmann's first crime is notorious I run some risk of purveying stale news. But for a younger generation it will suffice to mention the attempt of this enthusiast to blow up the German Crown Prince and suite when driving over Westminster Bridge on the occasion of their 1910 visit. Revenge for the severe measures taken against Berlin anarchists was the motive, but by some mischance the mine exploded just after the carriages had passed, wreaking, however, terrible havoc in the process. My sneer about the applewoman must not be taken too seriously, for though it is quite true that one such unfortunate perished, yet fifty to sixty victims fell with her in the crash of a rent arch. There was a terrible burst of indignation from all parts of the civilized world and the usual medley of useless arrests; the real culprits, Hartmann and his so-called 'shadow' Michael Schwartz, escaping to sea in a cargo-boat bound for Holland. The boat went down in a storm, and, failing further news, it was believed that all on board had gone down with her. Hartmann was known to have possessed large funds, and these also presumably lined the sea-bottom. Such was the official belief, and most people had agreed that the official belief was the right one.

I should add that among Hartmann's victims must, in a sense, be classed his mother. At the time of which I am now writing she was leading a very retired but useful life in Islington, where she spent her days in district-visiting and other charitable work. She still wore deep mourning, and had never, so it seemed, got over the shock caused by the appalling crime and early death of her son.

Burnett knew her very well indeed, though she scarcely appreciated his visits. I was myself on excellent terms with the old lady, but had not seen her for some weeks previous to the conversation here recorded. My time running fine, Burnett shortly rose to go.

"Be sure," he said, "and look me up early on your return. Mischief, I tell you, is brewing, and how soon I shall have to pitch my camp elsewhere I hardly know."

He was moving to the door when my landlady entered with a note. She had probably been listening to the conversation, for she glanced rather timorously at my guest before depositing her charge.

"Wait one moment, Burnett, and I'll see you out," said I, as I hastily broke the envelope. Yes, there was no mistaking the hand, the missive was really from my old friend, Mrs. Northerton. Its contents were fated to upset my programme. Only two days back I had arranged to meet the family in Paris at the express invitation of her husband, a genial old Liberal who took a lively interest in my work. This arrangement now received its death-blow.

3, Carshalton Terrace, Bayswater.

DEAR MR. STANLEY,
We have just returned from Paris, where we had, as you know, intended to stay some time. Old Mr. Matthews, whom you will recollect, died about a fortnight ago, leaving the Colonel one of his executors. As the estate is in rather a muddled condition, a good deal of attention may be necessary, so we made up our minds to forego the rest of our trip for the present. I shall be 'at home' to-morrow afternoon, when we shall be delighted to see you. With best wishes from all.
     Always yours sincerely,
      MAUDE C. NORTHERTON.
P.S. – Lena comes in for a bequest of £5000 in Mr. Matthews' will.

Lena in London! This was quite decisive.

"Excuse me, Burnett," I said, turning to my neglected friend; "but this letter is most important. A nice business pickle I am in, I can tell you."

"What nicely-scented notepaper your business correspondents use. You have my deep sympathies. Well, farewell for the present."

"Don't be in a hurry," I said; "I am afraid I must postpone this Continental trip after all. Business is business, whoever one's informant may be. No, I must really knock a few days off my rest."

Burnett stared, and concluded that something really serious was on hand.

"So you will be available for two or three days longer. That being so, I shall expect to see you at the old place about eight o'clock tomorrow evening. Be sure and come, for I have a guest with me of peculiar interest to both of us. His name? Oh! don't be impatient. It is a fixture, then? All right. No, I can't stay. Good-night."

I laughed heartily after I had seen him out. What a chequered life, what curious connections were mine – now a jostle with fashion, now with fanatics of anarchy like Burnett. Travelling, it is said, planes away social prejudices, and certainly in combination with Karl Marx it had done so in my case. Many friends used to rally me about my liking for the haunts of luxury, and some even went so far as to say it was of a piece with my other 'lukewarm' doctrines. The answer, however, was ready. I hated revolution, and I equally hated the pettiness of a sordid socialism. We must not, I contended, see the graces of high life, art and culture, fouled by the mob, but the mob elevated into a possession and appreciation of the graces. It was just because I believed some approach to this ideal to be possible that I fought under the banners of my party, and forewent travel and independence in the interests of the wage-slave. That I was no 'Orator Puff' I yearned for some opportunity to show. Cavillers would have then found that my money, my repute, and, if needful, my life, were all alike subservient to the cause I had at heart.

That night, however, lighter visions were to beguile my thoughts. When I dwelt upon once more meeting Miss Northerton, even Burnett's sombre hints lost their power to interest me. And when later on I did find time to sift them, they received short shrift at my hands. Bluster in large part, no doubt, was my verdict as I turned into bed that night. However, tomorrow I should be in a better position to judge. The interview would, at any rate, prove interesting, for Burnett's anarchist friends, however desperate, would furnish material in plenty for a student of human nature.

2. The Shadow of Hartmann

It was with a light heart that I made my way to the Northertons' the following afternoon. The prospect of a chat with the smart old gentleman and his ladies was delightful, and my only apprehensions concerned the assemblage I possibly might find there. As a rule receptions of this sort are tedious; prolific only of dyspepsia and boring conversations. Upper middle class mediocrity swarms round Mammon, and Mammon, the cult of the senses apart, is uninteresting. With Mill I was always of opinion that the thinker is corrupted by the pettinesses of ordinary 'social' intercourse. True, one occasionally meets a celebrity, but celebrities who are not professional talkers are best left unseen – their repute usually so outshines their deportment and conversation. Still, the celebrity is tolerable provided that not too much adulation is required. Happily, I rarely suffered at the Northertons. Ever and anon lions stalked through their premises, and the legions of well-to-do imbeciles thronged them. But there was generally the host or hostess to fall back upon, to say nothing of the companionship of Lena, to whom, if the secret must be revealed, I had for some time been engaged. The understanding was for the present to be privy to ourselves, but I had no reason to suppose that her worthy parents would have cause to object to the match. My politics, which might have scared most people of their standing, merely interested the ex-commissioner and were wholly indifferent to his wife. But still it was satisfactory to think that Lena would shortly come of age, and that our joint means would be sufficient to enable us to ignore any probable obstacles. Old Mr. Matthews' legacy had removed the last formidable barrier.

Two years before, I had the good fortune to meet the family on that memorable occasion when I was so hurriedly summoned from Egypt. The promenade deck of a P&O steamer offers boundless facilities for forming friendships, and during the brief interval which bridged my start from Suez and arrival at London, I was not slow in harvesting these advantages to the full. Old Mr. Northerton was returning home after serving his time in the Indian Civil Service, and with him were his wife, his two sons, and an only daughter. My singular interest in the family hinged mainly on the latter, a charming young girl of some eighteen summers. What that interest culminated in I have already said. It only remains to add that the cordial relations set up between the family and myself were never allowed to drop. The two sons were now serving on the Indian Staff Corps, but I corresponded with them over and anon, and even reckoned the younger among my numerous socialist proselytes. Old Northerton was well aware of this, and though himself a Liberal of the old school, had no reproach for the teacher. After all a 'sub' reading Karl Marx under the 'punkahs of Dum-Dum' was scarcely a formidable convert.

A short walk carried me to the terrace, and ere long I was being warmly greeted by the only three available members of the family. Mrs. Northerton was too busy with her guests to pay me much attention, so after a few explanations and regrets for the spoilt trip, I was borne off in charge of the genial commissioner.

"Well, how go your election prospects?" he said, as cheerily as if my programme favoured his class.

"Not as well as I could wish. They say I am too moderate for the constituency. You know, of course, that Lawler, a 'blood and thunder' tub-thumper, is standing against me in the interests of the extreme party."

"So I hear, but I should scarcely have thought he would have stood a chance."

"On the contrary, I assure you he speaks for a

numerous and very ugly party – a party which arrears of legislation have done as much as anything to create. Talking of this, I am not at all sure that we may not have trouble before long. I shall do my best to have the peace kept, but there's no knowing to what the more reckless agitators may drive the mob."

"There I agree with you, sir," broke in an acute-looking old gentleman with spectacles; "but how do you reconcile that opinion with your own doctrines? How can you speak and write for socialism when you grumble at its practical enforcement? You state that you oppose revolution, but is a constitutional settlement of the problem possible?"

"Why not? You must remember that large sections of socialists are against revolution. Looking back at the graduated nature of the transition between feudalism and modern capitalism, these men would meditate, if possible, a similar though perhaps more rapid transition between modern capitalism and socialism. Any sudden metamorphosis of society would, they believe, breed appalling evils. I am quite of this way of thinking myself."

My interlocutor laughed. He evidently thought me a reasonable enough creature for my kind. The commissioner remarked that it was a pity that all the party were not of my way of thinking.

"But," I added, "I have no hesitation in saying that

if I thought a revolution would pay, for revolution I would declare myself. It is only a question of cost complicated by dangers of reaction and anarchy. The consideration which weighs most with me is the difficulty of organizing and legislating at a time when panic and brutality would be rampant. I know no men competent to stand at the helm in such tempests. Even with civil peace to help us, a settlement would require, to my thinking, years of patient labour. Mere revolutionary conventions, with some ready-made constitution and brand-new panaceas for suffering, would be impotent."

"Impotent," echoed the old gentleman. "By the way, you have not answered my question."

"The object, sir, of my agitation is to force the projected reforms on public attention, and so to secure that most important of allies, an effective mob-backing. But let me add that once elected to Parliament I am prepared to stand by any Government, Tory or Radical, in supporting the cause of order. We contend that should the revolutionary socialists or the anarchists initiate a crusade in the streets, they must take the consequences of their temerity."

"Well said," observed the ex-commissioner. "I notice in this regard that some very disquieting rumours are afloat. Not only are many of the East and South London workers becoming dangerous, but these miscreants, the anarchists, are moving. You remember the fiendish massacre ten years back when Hartmann blew up the bridge?"

"Rather."

"Well, the police have had information that this wretch is not dead after all. At the present moment he is believed to be in England stirring up more mischief."

"The deuce he is!" cried the old gentleman. "I hope they will run him to earth."

At this point our colloquy was broken off by Lena, who sailed gracefully through the crowd.

"I want you for a moment, Mr. Stanley. A friend of mine, Mrs. Gryffyn, is very anxious to make your acquaintance. She's mad about land law reform and women's suffrage."

The old gentleman grinned and Mr. Northerton eyed me pityingly. There was no escape from the inquisitor. "Why on earth couldn't you spare me this, Lena?" I whispered. "I want a talk with you all alone, not an hour with this virago."

"Oh, it's all right. I shall keep you company, and as she is going soon we shall be able to get into a quiet nook and have a long chat."

The ordeal over, I had the luxury of a tête-à-tête with my fiancée, and excellent use I made of the limited time at my disposal. I was very fond of Lena, who was not only a charmingly pretty girl, but, thank goodness! sympathized most cordially with the bulk of my political opinions. She never of course mixed with the peculiar circles I frequented, but dearly loved to follow my reports of the movements which they represented. The only person remotely connected with them she knew was Mrs. Hartmann, to whose house I had brought her in the hope that the old lady might find a friend. Lena was often to be seen in the little parlour at Islington, and knew probably more about the poor widow's troubles than any one else. As her parents gave her complete freedom of action, she had plenty of opportunities for cultivating the acquaintance. After our private confidences had been duly exchanged, the conversation naturally drifted to this topic. I was anxious to know about the old lady's welfare, and casually mentioned the rumour which concerned her son. Had it reached her ears?

"I am sure I don't know," said Lena; "she seemed in marvellously good spirits when I saw her last, but she made no allusion whatever to the subject. How could she, when you come to think of it? It is all very well rejoicing over a prodigal son's return, but this son was a fiend, and would be much better lying quiet at the bottom of the sea, where people imagined him."

"But you forget, dear, that he was her only son, and always good to her."

"That's true, but look at the blood on his hands.

By the bye, Mrs. Hartmann once told me the whole story. Hartmann, you know, was educated for the profession of an engineer, and was always looked on as a prodigy of intellectual vigour. Whatever he did he did well, and as he came into a considerable fortune when of age, a brilliant career was predicted for him. Mrs. Hartmann says that at that time she never knew he had any other interests than those of his calling, but it appears from later discoveries that when twenty-three years of age he made the acquaintance of a German exile, one Schwartz, a miscreant of notorious opinions and character. This man gradually inspired him with a hatred of the whole fabric of society, and the end of it was that he became an anarchist. That Hartmann was deeply in earnest seems perfectly clear. He sacrificed to his aim, position, comfort, reputation, his studies – in short, everything. He regarded civilization as rotten from top to foundation, and the present human race as 'only fit for fuel.' Schwartz was a pessimist, and his pupil became one of an even deeper dye."

"But what was his ultimate aim?"

"He thought, like some eighteenth-century writers, that man must revert to simpler conditions of life and make a new start. He hoped, so his mother says, that his example would fire the minds of others, and so topple over the very pedestals of governments and law. It was absurd, he held, for a few men to war against society, but, he added, the affection he laboured under was catching. He trusted that one day London and the great cities of Europe would be in ruins."

"But," I interposed, "this is fanaticism, or rather madness. It is a disease bred by an effete form of civilization. Is this all the wily anarchist plotted for?"

"Well, it's a pretty large 'all', is it not? By the way, he had one persistent craze, the belief in some invention which would one day place society at his mercy."

"So? Awkward that for society."

We talked for some time longer, when I called my appointment to mind, and tearing myself away from my kind friends sallied forth into the street. It was not easy to refuse the ex-commissioner's invitation to dinner in view of Burnett's dismal parlour at Stepney. Still I was not a little interested in his guest, and anxious, as far as possible, to keep Burnett himself out of mischief. Hitherto he had been a mere theorist with a very kindly side, and there seemed no reason why, with care, he should not remain one. But he required, so I thought, watching. With these thoughts uppermost in my mind I hailed a hansom, and ordered the driver to drop me in the East End in a road running hard by the anarchist's house.

I can recall my entrance into that parlour most vividly. Burnett had let me in with his usual caution.

Whisking off my coat I followed him to the parlour. There was a bright burning in the grate, and the gleam of the flames – the only light in the room – lit up a whisky-bottle and some glasses on the table, and ever and anon revealed the rude prints on the walls and the rough deal shelves heaped with books. Everything smelt of the practical. In the place of the Louis XIV furniture of the Northertons, only a wooden table and some three or four deal chairs met the eye, the sole article rejoicing in a cushion being a rudely-carved sofa in the corner. The single window, I noticed, was carefully curtained and barred. Stepping toward the mantelpiece, Burnett struck a match, and proceeded to light a couple of candles which crowned that dusty eminence.

I then saw to my surprise that we were not alone. On a chair by the left-hand corner of the fire sat an elderly man apparently of the higher artisan class. His face was most unprepossessing. There was a bull-dog's obstinacy and attachment about it, but the eyes were unspeakably wicked and the mouth hard and cruel. I diagnosed it at once as that of a man whose past was best unread, whose hand had in dark by-ways been persistently raised against his fellow men. It takes time to analyze this impression, but originally it seized me in a moment. I was prejudiced, accordingly, at the outset, but judge of my astonishment and disgust when

Burnett cried, "Here, Schwartz, is my old pal Stanley." It was the shameless miscreant known as the shadow of Hartmann!

Coldly enough I took the proffered hand. So this was the fanatic supposed to be long ago dead. One felt like abetting a murderer.

"Stanley seems startled," laughed Burnett. "He is not much accustomed to high life. Come, man, acknowledge you had a surprise."

The meeting was half of my seeking, and decency after all forbade openly expressed dislike. Besides, Schwartz was in practice only what Burnett was in theory, and what possibly even I and other moderates might become at a pinch.

"I confess," I replied, "I was taken somewhat aback. It is seldom the sea gives up its dead, and one does not meet celebrities like Herr Schwartz every day."

Schwartz laughed grimly. I could see he was pleasantly tickled. Monstrous conceits sprout from the shedding of blood. He seemed to chuckle that he, outcast and rebel, had hurled so many of his fellows into nothingness. If this was the man, what of the master?

"Fill up your glass, Stanley," and Burnett pushed the whisky across the table. "Sit down and ask what questions you like."

Schwartz looked me carefully over.

"You say again that you answer for this friend," he muttered to Burnett.

"As I would for myself."

"It is well."

"Hartmann is alive then," I ventured, "after all?"

"Very much so," put in Burnett. "The most he got was a wetting. He and Schwartz were picked up by a fishing-boat and carried to Dieppe. Hence they made their way to Switzerland, where they have been for some years. Hartmann had money, Schwartz devotion. Money bred money – they grew rich, and they will yet lead anarchy to triumph, for at last, after long years of danger, delay, and disappointment, the dream of Hartmann is realized!"

My companions exchanged meaningful glances. Evidently they were in high spirits.

"And the deputy, the socialist, will he join us?" cried Schwartz. "He will have no struggles, no dangers; he will tread capital underfoot; he will raise his hand, and fortresses will rattle around him."

Both the anarchists broke into renewed laughter. I was tired of hyperbole and wished to get at the facts. But do what I would my men refused to be 'squeezed'. For a long time I could only glean from them that Hartmann was in London, and plotting mischief on some hitherto unimagined scale. At last I grew irritated at the splutter.

"Nonsense, Herr Schwartz, nonsense! Stir a step worth the noting and the very workers will rise and crush you. I tell you your notions are fantastic, your campaign against society maniacal. How can a few scattered incendiaries or dynamiters, ceaselessly dodging the law, hope to defy a state? The thing is ridiculous. As well match a pop-gun against a 'Woolwich infant'."

"My friend speaks of a struggle such as one man might wage against a mob in the street. It is not for this that Hartmann has plotted so long. It is not to be shot by soldiers or hunted by police that he will once more shake this city. Do you wish to guess his weapon? Take this piece of stuff in your hand, and tell me what you think of it."

As he spoke he rummaged his pockets and produced a small plate, apparently of silvery grey metal, of about two square inches of surface, and one-tenth of an inch or so in thickness. I examined it carefully.

"Now take this steel knife and hammer and test its hardness and texture." I did so. Burnett looked on knowingly.

"Well, it is extremely tough and hard, for I can make no impression. What it is, however, I can't say."

"But its weight, its weight!" said Burnett.

I must have changed colour.

"Why, it is as light or lighter than cardboard. What an extraordinary combination of attributes!"

"Extraordinary indeed! It is the grandest of Hartmann's strokes! But you cannot guess its use?"

I shook my head.

"Well, suppose you try to think it out between now and Saturday night, when I will promise to introduce you to the inventor himself."

"What, Hartmann?"

"Yes; let us see, you are to address a meeting down at Turner's Hall in this quarter on Saturday. I will be in the audience, and we will beard the captain in company. Midnight, Kensington Gardens, by the pond to the left as you enter from the Queen's Road – that is the rendezvous. Come, are you ready? I think I may tell you that you will run no risks, while at any rate you will see something strange beyond compare."

I hesitated, the mystery was deepening, and to confront and "have it out" with the celebrated, if hateful, anarchist, would be interesting. And these queer hints too?

"Yes, I'm your man; but we must have no companions – for obvious reasons."

Burnett nodded. Shortly afterwards the obnoxious German took his departure and left us to ourselves. I am not sure that he quite trusted my intentions, for the dread of the police spy was ever present with him.

We two talked on till midnight. On rising to go I made a final effort to 'squeeze' the anarchist.

"Come, John, it's no use playing the mystery man any longer. I shall know everything by Saturday night, or rather Sunday morning. You trust me with your other secrets, trust me with this; at any rate, a three days' interval can't make much difference."

Burnett thought a moment, stepped to his shelves, and took down a work of somewhat antique binding. It was from the pen of a nineteenth-century savant of high repute in his day. Slowly, and without comment, he read me the following passage :- "Yet there is a real impediment in the way of man navigating the air, and that is the excessive weight of the only great mechanical moving powers hitherto placed at his disposal. When science shall have discovered some moving power greatly lighter than any we yet know, in all probability the problem will be solved."

The silvery grey substance had solved it!

3. A Mother's Troubles

A raw London morning is a terrible foe to romance – visions that have danced elf-like before the view on the foregoing night tend to lose their charm or even to merge themselves wholly in the commonplace. So it was with me. When I came down to breakfast and reviewed the situation calmly, I was ready to laugh at my faith in what seemed the wild vagaries of Schwartz and Burnett. The memory of the queer little parlour and its queerer tenants had lost its overnight vividness and given place to a suspicion that either I or my hosts had indulged too freely in whisky. The little plate, however, was still in my possession, and this very tangible witness sufficed, despite a growing scepticism, to give me pause. 'A striking discovery no doubt,' was my verdict, 'but the dream of Hartmann, as Burnett calls it, is not so easily realized.' Still I should know all – if anything worth the mention was to be known – on Saturday night if I showed up at the odd trysting-place named by Burnett – a trysting-place which at that hour meant a scramble over palings, and possible trouble with the police. But these things were trifles. All things considered, I should do well to present myself with or without Burnett, for the boasted aëronef apart, the threats of the anarchists had begun to perplex me mightily, and the wish to meet their notorious leader, the so terrible son of my old friend Mrs. Hartmann, was not to be summarily exorcised.

I had passed the morning in study. Luncheon over, I jotted down some notes for my speech on the following Saturday. Next, I sent Lena a note promising to look in on Sunday afternoon, sallied out with it to the post, and then ensconced myself in an omnibus which was plying in the direction of Islington. Whither was I bound? For the house of my friend Mrs. Hartmann, whom, as already mentioned, I had not seen for some time, and whose conversation just now might be fraught with peculiar interest. Had the son as yet seen the mother? Had any inkling of these vaguely discussed new plots reached her? Had she any clue to the overnight mystery? Questions such as these surged up in dozens, and I determined, if possible, to feel my way to their answers.

It was late in the afternoon when I reached Mrs. Hartmann's modest villa in Islington. The maid who admitted me said that she was not at home, having gone to visit a sick child in the neighbourhood. She expected her back to tea, and meanwhile perhaps I would like to wait. There was clearly no resource open to me but to do so, and entering the narrow hall I was shown into a drawing-room, simply but withal not uncomfortably furnished. The bay window which lighted the apartment looked on to a neat grass plot diversified by some small but well-kept parterres.

There was little within to catch the eye. Exploring the walls I came across a shelf full of musty books, mathematical and engineering text-books, and a variety of treatises on political economy and the sciences, evidently mementos of the son! While glancing through some and noting the numerous traces of careful study, the thought struck me that the photograph of their misguided possessor might also be accessible. I had been many times in the room before, but had never been favoured with the old lady's confidences on the score of her son. The wound caused by his crime was ever green, and I, at least, was not cruel enough to disturb it. However, being now left alone I resolved to consult her albums, which, at any rate, might serve to while away the hour. Loosening the clasp of one that lay near to hand, I turned over its leaves rapidly. As a rule, I dislike collections of this sort; there is a prosiness peculiar to albums which forbids incautious research. But here the hunt was of interest. True, there were mediocre denizens in plenty, shoals of cousins, sisters, and aunts, hordes of nonentities whom Burnett would have dubbed only 'fit for fuel,' but there was one discoverable and very satisfactory tenant – a loose photograph marked on its back, 'R. Hartmann, taken when twenty-three years of age,' just about the time of the celebrated bridge incident.

It was the face of a young man evidently of high capacity and unflinching resolution. A slight moustache brushed the upper lip, and set off a clear-cut but somewhat cruel mouth. A more completely independent expression I never saw. The lineaments obscured by time defied accurate survey, but the general effect produced was that they indicated an arbitrary and domineering soul, utterly impatient of control and loftily contemptuous of its kind.

I was carefully conning the face when I heard the garden-gate creak on its hinges, a sound followed by the rattle of a latch-key in the lock of the front door. Mrs. Hartmann had returned. Passing into the room, she met me with a pleasant smile which showed up in curious contrast to the look of depression so familiar to me of yore. I interpreted that brightness in an instant. Hartmann had returned, and had paid her the visit of one raised from the dead. But of his terrible designs, of his restless hatred of society, he had clearly told her nothing.

Hers was an expressive face, and the shadows upon it were few enough to warrant that inference. Probably he had smoothed over the past and fooled her with some talk of a reformed life and a changed creed. It is so easy for an only son to persuade a mother – particularly when he rises after long years from a supposed grave.

"Well, Mr. Stanley, you are the last person I expected to see. I heard you were to be in Paris today."

"So, my dear Mrs. Hartmann, I was, but the Northertons, you see, have returned, and I had hoped to have done some touring with the old gentleman."

"Or perhaps with Miss Lena. No, don't look so innocent, for she tells me more than you think. But what of this return? I had a note from her when she was in Paris, but she said nothing about it?"

"Some will business," I explained. "You will be glad to hear she comes in for £5000 by it."

"A nice little nest-egg to begin house-keeping upon. I think, Mr. Stanley, you two young people ought to do very well."

"I hope so," I said, foregoing useless secrecy – what a chatterbox Lena could be! "At any rate I see no very dangerous rocks ahead at present."

The conversation wandered for some time among various topics, when I mentioned that I had been looking over the album.

"And very stupid work you must have found it," she said.

"Oh, it kept me busy while waiting. By the way, one of the photographs is loose," and I handed her that of her son, this time with the face upwards. The ruse was effective, and the conversation took the desired course.

"Have you never seen that face before? It is that of Rudolf, my misguided son, of whom you must have heard. Poor boy! Ten years have rolled by since his death."

Admirably cool this mother; she at least was not to be 'squeezed' offhand. But my watched-for chance had come.

"My dear Mrs. Hartmann, he is alive, and you know it. Two days ago he was in this very house."
I had drawn my bow at a venture, but the shaft served me well. The coup was decisive. The old lady's face betrayed complete discomfiture mingled with obvious signs of alarm. She made no attempt to contradict me.

"What!" she stammered out at length. "Are you also in the secret? Are you, too, one of –"

"No," I replied bluntly, anticipating her meaning. "I have never met your son, though I know something perhaps of his movements. But believe me you may trust me as you would yourself.

He was a 'dynamitard', but he is your son, and that is enough for me. Rest assured of my silence."

Her distress visibly abated.

"Thanks, many thanks. I feel I can rely on you – even to lend him a helping hand should the time ever come. Ah! he is a changed man, an entirely changed man. A bright future may await him even now across the sea. But this visit to me – so sudden, so brief – I fear lest it may cost him dear. You, a private man, have found it out; why may not the lynx-eyed police also? It is terrible, this suspense. How can I be sure that he is safe at this moment?"

"Oh, as to that, happily I can reassure you. Your son is safe enough – nay, as safe as the most anxious mother could desire. How or where I cannot say, but I have it on the best possible authority. In fact, only last night I heard as much from the lips of one who should surely know – Michael Schwartz himself!"

"That evil genius! Is he too in London? Ah! if he is content, all is well. No tigress ever watched better over her cub than Schwartz over my son. Would his likings had blown elsewhere! That man was my son's tutor in vice. But for him, Rudolf might have been an honour to his country. And what is he now? An outlaw, in the shadow of the gallows…" and she hid her face in her handkerchief and wept bitterly. I waited patiently till the tempest was over, putting in a soothing phrase here and there and painting black white with the zeal of a skilful casuist. One need not be too scrupulous when sufferers such as this are concerned.

"He has told you nothing of his movements?" I remarked cautiously.

"Nothing, except that he was leaving shortly for Hamburg, whence he was to proceed immediately to New York. Some months later on I may join him there, but for the present all is uncertain." One more deception of Hartmann's, but a kindly one; obviously it was better not to disturb the illusions which the old lady thus fondly cherished – her reformed son, his prospective honourable life, the vision of a lasting reunion abroad. Were she to suspect that mischief was again being plotted by the anarchist, what a cruel scattering of her hopes would follow!

I assured her that the chances were all in her son's favour, and that once in America he could set at naught all possibilities of discovery. Meanwhile, I had become aware that nothing of importance to my quest was to be drawn from Mrs. Hartmann. Her son's meteoric visit, prompted by some gleam of noble sentiment, had evidently left her ignorant of his new inhuman plottings. Ere long I rose to leave, not, however, without having promised that, should Hartmann ever cross my path, I would stand by him for her sake in a possible hour of danger. Under what circumstances I was to meet this extraordinary man – how absurd then my poor well-meant promise of assistance was to appear – will be manifest from the ensuing narrative.

4. Fugitives from the Law

On Saturday evening I addressed a stormy meeting at Stepney. Since I bade adieu to Mrs. Hartmann much had occurred to rouse the sleeping tigers in the country. Riots had been reported from many great towns, while handbills of the most violent sort were being thrust on the workers of London. Revolutionary counsels had been long scattered by a thousand demagogues, and it appeared now that the ingathering of the harvest was nigh. A renewal of anarchist outrages had terrorized the well-to-do and fanned the extremists into vehemence. A terrible explosion was reported from Kensington, three houses, including that of the Home Secretary, Mr. Baynton, having been completely wrecked, while ten of their inmates had been killed and some fourteen more or less severely injured. A disastrous catastrophe had been narrowly averted from the Mansion House. It may be imagined, therefore, that it was with a grave face that I ascended the platform that evening; my course being rendered so difficult by reason of the extremists – on the one hand by the Conservatives, who, to my thinking, were perpetuating the conditions whence anarchy drew its breath, namely, a wretched proletariat exploited by capital; on the other by the extreme socialists, who despaired of effective advance by way of ordinary parliamentary reforms. Both parties were strongly represented that night, and, political feeling running so high, the prospect of an orderly meeting seemed shadowy. I had some unpleasant truths to press home, and was not to be deterred from this duty.

Before rising to speak I glanced anxiously around the hall, and imagine my feelings when I found that Burnett was missing. This breach of his engagement was ominous. That he had a hand in the outrages was possible – his tone had of late been most threatening, and the influence of Schwartz was malefic – though the supposition was one I did not like to entertain. At any rate he might well have been suspected of complicity, and forced to seek refuge in flight. It was with a heavy heart that I obeyed the behest of the chairman and rose to address the meeting.

What I said matters little. Severe condemnation of the outrages, a sharp critique of the individualist-Conservative groups, an appeal for unity and order in our agitation, were the points upon which I laid emphasis. I had spoken for about half an hour when my audience refused to let me proceed. Previously to this, interruptions had been frequent, but now a violent uproar arose, the uproar led to a fight, and a rush was made for the platform, which, albeit gallantly defended, was speedily enough stormed. I had the pleasure of knocking over one ruffian who leapt at me brandishing a chair, but a brutal kick from behind sent me spinning into the crush by the steps. Severely cuffed and pommelled, I was using my fists freely when the gas was suddenly turned off, and the struggle being summarily damped, I managed somehow to get into the street.

And now came the exciting business of the night. In the mass of shouting enthusiasts outside it was useless to look for Burnett. I determined, therefore, to track him down to his own quarters. Passing back into the committee-room I hastily scribbled some rather indignant lines to my chairman, and then pulling my hat over my eyes elbowed my way through the press.

By the time I got clear of the street I was considerably flushed and heated, and the rate at which I was going by no means conduced to refresh me. After ten minutes' sharp walk I plunged down the narrow street where Burnett's house lay, and a few seconds later had kicked back the gate and marched

up to the door. I was startled to find it ajar. Burnett
was so habitually cautious that I knew something must
be amiss. Pushing it slowly open I stole noiselessly
into the passage and glanced through the keyhole of
the door which led into the little parlour. It was well
I had not tramped in. Two policemen and a man in
plain clothes were standing round a hole in the floor,
and the whole apartment was strewn with prized-up
planks. On a chair close by was a heap of retorts,
bottles, and canisters, while three ugly-looking bombs
lay on the hearthstone.

Burnett, then, had really been mixed up in these
outrages, and the police were on his trail, if indeed
they had not already arrested him. And what about
my own position? The best thing for me was to make
off in a trice, for the entanglements, troubles, and
disgrace in which capture there would plunge me
were too appalling to contemplate. Instantly I glided
to the door, and gently – this time – revolving the gate,
slipped out hurriedly into the street. Fortunately there
was no one on watch, or my arrest would have been
speedy. As it was I rapidly gained the main street and
was soon lost in the broad stream of pedestrians.

Having still three hours before me, I turned into a
confectioner's, and over a substantial tea endeavoured
to think the matter out. That I was furious with Burnett
goes without saying.

Only his fanatical theories separated him to my mind from the common murderer. But that he should be caught was a thought utterly revolting, for I had liked the man warmly, and had owed my life to his pluck. No; our friendship must cease henceforth, but it was at least my duty to warn him, if still at large, of the discovery. But how? There was only one course open to me. Outrages or no outrages, police or no police, I must be present at the meeting in the park that night. It was quite possible that Burnett, ignorant of the search made at his house, might be still strolling about London, a prize for the first aspiring police officer who should meet him. Yes, I would go and chance meeting the group, for I should mention that the exact spot for the rendezvous was unknown to me. All I knew was that it was somewhere near the pond to the left as you enter from the Queen's Road. The best thing I could think of was to idle outside the park, until I could climb the palings unnoticed.

The sky was overcast with clouds, and so far the project was favoured. Hazardous as was the affair, my resolution was speedily made and fortified. Leaving the shop I sallied out for a stroll and passed the remaining interval as best I could. Then I called for a hansom, and, leaping in, ordered the driver to take me to the Marble Arch. He demurred at first, saying the journey was too much for his horse at that time of night, but his scruples were silenced by the offer of a half-sovereign for his pains. The mute objections of his steed were quashed with a sharp cut of the whip, and I was whirled swiftly on to an adventure which was to beggar the wildest creations of romance.

At the Marble Arch I dismissed the cab and walked briskly along the Hyde Park side in the direction of Notting Hill. I had gone some few hundred yards when a hansom sped by me rapidly, and a well-known face within it flashed on my vision like a meteor. It was Burnett, of all persons! Shouting and waving my stick I rushed wildly in chase of the vehicle, and, by dint of desperate efforts, succeeded at last in stopping it. As I approached the window, the trap flew up.

"Drive on, man, drive on, never mind," growled a hoarse voice, and I heard the click of a revolver.

"Here I am," I said, getting on the step and rapping the window just as the man was about to whip up. Burnett stared.

"What, you here!" he said, flinging apart the leaves. "Come in quick. I don't know who may be behind." I mounted in a trice, and the cab flew on faster than ever.

"Look here," I said, breathlessly, "I have come to warn you. The police are on your track."

"I know it, my boy," he rejoined, "but I think they have some way to run yet. No fear. I leave London in an hour."

What was the man talking of – was he raving, or boasting, or what?

"Hi, stop!" We got out, and the cab rolled away complacently.

"Now over the palings," cried Burnett. "You will see Hartmann?"

"Yes, for an instant." The demon of curiosity was urgent, and the coast seemed clear.

"All right. Come, sharp."

It was no easy task for me, tired as I was, but with the help of my companion I got through it somehow.

"Hallo! Look!" A second cab (probably informed by ours) was bearing down rapidly with two occupants, one of whom stood excitedly on the steps. "Detectives! We're spotted!" I leapt to the ground desperately. Heavens! where had my curiosity landed me?

"Put your best leg foremost and follow me," yelled Burnett, and his revolver flashed in the gas-light.

In my foolish excitement I obeyed him. As we rushed along I heard the men leap out and their boots clink on the iron of the palings. I felt like the quarry of the wild huntsman of German legend. If arrested in such a plight, and in such company, a deluge of disgrace, if not worse, awaited me. I ran like a deer from a leopard, but I felt I could not hold out very long at so break-neck a speed.

"Keep – your – pecker – up," shouted Burnett brokenly.

"Hartmann – is – waiting."

"To be arrested with us," was my thought, or was more murder imminent? God! how I cursed my foolhardiness and useless sacrifice!

"Here – we are – at last!" cried my companion, looking back over his shoulder. "One – effort – more."

Half dizzy with fear and fatigue I made a despairing sprint, when, my foot striking a root, I was hurled violently to the ground. All I remember is seeing two dusky forms rushing up, and Burnett hurriedly wheeling round. Then from some unknown spot broke a salvo of cracks of revolvers. A heavy body fell bleeding across my face, and almost at once consciousness left me.

5. A Strange Awakening

Where was I? I seemed to be escaping from the throes of some horrible dream, with a headache past endurance. I stretched out my right hand and it struck something cold and hard. I opened one eye with an effort, and I saw three men bending over me as one sees spectres in a nightmare. Slowly there was borne upon me the sound of voices, and then the cruel remembrance of that struggle. I was in a police cell, and might have to expiate my misfortunes with shame or even death. Who was to believe my tale? Horrified at the thought, I gave utterance to a deep groan.

"There's not much up with your pal, Jack," said one of the spectres aforesaid; "give him some more whisky; he's hit his head and got knocked silly, that's all."

What was this? A surge of blood coursed through me. I made a supreme effort and opened both eyes fully. The light was poor, but it was enough.

The face of the man nearest me was the face of Burnett, by him stood a rough-looking artisan, and, by all that is marvellous, Michael Schwartz!

"Here, take this," said Burnett, as the rough-looking man handed him the glass, "you'll be all right in a minute." I drank it off mechanically and, imbued with new strength, sat bolt upright on the bench. Burnett watched me satirically as I tried to cope with the situation. By the light of a small lamp hanging in a niche over my head I saw that I was in a low small room about twelve feet square, with bare greyish-looking walls and a few slit-like openings near the ceiling which did duty, no doubt, for windows. A few chests, several chairs, and a table of the same greyish colour constituted its furniture. Almost directly opposite me was a low door through which blew gusts of chilly mist, but as to what lay beyond it I could not of course form a conjecture. Having made this rapid survey I turned in astonishment to my three stolid companions, mutely entreating some sort of clue to the mystery.

Schwartz then made an attempt to rouse me by asking how I had enjoyed my nocturnal run in the park. But I was still too surprised to answer. I was thinking how Burnett could have carried me safe away, where he could possibly have brought me, what had become of our pursuers, where the mysterious Hartmann was, who had fired the shots?

These and a multitude of like riddles rendered me speechless with bewilderment. When I had more or less fully regained voice and strength I turned to Burnett, and ignoring the impish Schwartz, said curtly –

"Where on earth am I?"

"You aren't on earth at all," was the answer, and the three burst into a hearty laugh. "Nor in heaven," added the speaker; "for if so neither Schwartz nor Thomas would be near you."

"Come, a truce to humbug! Am I in London, on the river, in an anarchist's haunt, or where?"

"I am quite serious. But if you want something more explicit, well, you are not in London but above it."

I looked at the three wonderingly. A faint light was beginning to break on my mind. But no, the thing was impossible!

"Are you able to walk now?" said Burnett. "Come, Schwartz, you take one arm and I'll take another. Between us we'll give Mr. Constitutionalist a lesson. Stanley, my boy, in all your days you never saw a sight such as I am going to show you now."

"But it is nothing to what we shall see, comrade, when the captain gives the word," added Schwartz.

"Thank you," I replied, "I will lean on you, Burnett. I can do without Herr Schwartz's assistance."

We moved across the room.

"Shh!" whispered Burnett, "don't be nasty to the German.

He's the captain's right hand. It was he, too, who knocked over your man just now and so saved you from trouble. Take my advice and be discreet."

I nodded.

"But who –"

"Wait a moment and look around you."

We had crossed the doorway and were standing in a sort of open bulwarked passage which evidently ran for some length on either side. I stepped to the bulwarks.

"Look below," said Burnett.

I looked long and earnestly, while Schwartz and Thomas stood silently in the background. It was a strange sight, and it was some time ere I seized its meaning. It was very dark outside, the only light being that coming through the doorway of the chamber I had just quitted. But far below, as it seemed, glittered innumerable specks like stars, a curious contrast to the inkiness of the cloudy pall above us. As I gazed down into the depths I became conscious of a dull murmur like that of whirling machinery, and forthwith detected a constant vibration of the ledge on which my elbow rested. Then, and then only, the truth rushed upon me.

I was being carried over London in the craft of Hartmann the Anarchist.

Horrified with my thoughts – for the potentialities of

this fell vessel dazed me – I clung fiercely to Burnett's arm.

"I am, then, on the…" I gasped.

"Deck of the Attila," put in Burnett. "Behold the craft that shall wreck civilization and hurl tyrannies into nothingness!"

But my gaze was fixed on those lights far below, and my thought was not of the tyrannies I had left, but of the tyranny this accursed deck might minister to. And Hartmann, they said, was remorseless.

"Yes," growled Thomas hoarsely, "I live for the roar of the dynamite."

Schwartz, stirred to enthusiasm, shouted a brutal parody of Tennyson:

The dynamite falls on castle walls
And splendid buildings old in story.
The column shakes, the tyrant quakes,
And the wild wreckage leaps in glory.
Throw, comrade, throw: Set the wild echoes flying;
Throw, comrade; Answer, wretches,
Dying, dying, dying.

If the remainder of the crew resembled this sample, I was caged in a veritable inferno. As yet, of course, I knew nothing of their numbers or feelings, but my expectations were far from being roseate.

"But, man!" I cried, turning to Burnett, "would you

massacre helpless multitudes? You, who prate of tyranny, would you, also, play the role of tyrants?"

Before the gathering horror all my wonder at the Attila had vanished. I felt only the helpless abject dismay with which one confronts an appalling but inevitable calamity. At that moment some disaster to the aëronef would have been welcome. The masterful vice of the fanatics maddened me. Rebel, however, as I might, I was of no account. The snake that snapped at the file had more in his favour.

"We don't argue here," said Burnett, "we act. If you want arguments, you must wait till you see the captain. Disputes with us are useless."

So even he was becoming surly. It was natural enough, however, as a moment's reflection showed. The alligator on land is ordinarily mild enough, in his element he is invariably a terrible monster. The "suspect" anarchist of Stepney was courteous and argumentative, but the free and independent anarchist of the Attila dogmatic and brutal. It was obviously best policy to humour him, for he alone, perhaps, might stand by me at a pinch. I endeavoured to throw oil on the troubled waters.

"You used not to mind criticism," I urged.

"Oh no! but those days are past. Don't take what I say unkindly, for we all mean you well. The captain will always talk, but we here are tired of it.

We only exist now to act – when the word is passed. So you will consult our convenience and your own much more effectually if you drop all such homilies for the future."

"Yes," put in Thomas, "I had enough of it in London. Fifteen years of revolutionary socialist talking and nothing ever done! But wait a few weeks and I warrant it will be said that we here have atoned wonderfully well for arrears. Come, a glass to our captain – the destined destroyer of civilization!"

The gallant three, acting on this hint, left me to digest their advice and retired within. How long I remained thinking I know not. Someone brought me a chair, but I was too abstracted to thank him. For fully an hour I must have looked down on those twinkling lights with a terror beyond the power of words to express. All was as Burnett had said. The dream of Hartmann was realized. The exile and outcast, lately sheltered from the law in the shadow of Continental cities, now enjoyed power such as a hundred Czars could not hope for. The desperadoes with him, hated by and hating society, were probably one and all devoured by lust of blood and revenge. The three I knew were all proscribed men, loathing not only the landlord and capitalist but the workers, who would most of them have rejoiced over their capture. They attacked not only the abuses and the defects but the very foundations of society. Their long-cherished thought had been to shatter the trophies of centuries. And the long-contemplated opportunity had come at last!

One resource remained. What they meant to do with me was uncertain. But my relations with Burnett and the friendship of Hartmann's mother were sufficient to avert any apprehension of violence. My endeavour then henceforward must be to work on the mind of Hartmann, to divert this engine of mischief into as fair a course as possible, to achieve by its aid a durable and relatively bloodless social revolution, and to reap by an authority so secure from overthrow a harvest of beneficial results. Buoyed up by these brighter thoughts, I now began to find time for a more immediate interest. What of this wonderful vessel or aëronef itself? What was it built of? How was it propelled, supported, steered, manned, constructed? Rising from my chair, I felt my way forward along the railing, but found the way barred by some door or partition. As I made my way back I met Burnett, who emerged from the low door already mentioned.

"What, exploring already?" he said. "It's no good at this hour, as you have doubtless discovered. Come inside and I'll see you are made cosy for the night. You must want sleep, surely."

I followed him in without a word. Passing into the chamber he pressed a spring in the wall, and a concealed door flew back revealing a dark recess. He struck a light, and there became visible a comfortable berth with the usual appurtenances of a homely cabin such as one would occupy in the second-class saloon of an ordinary ocean-going steamer.

"By the way," I said, "you have not told me what happened in the park; I am dying to know."

"It is easily told. When you fell, the two detectives were up in a moment. I turned round meaning to shoot, but before I emptied a barrel, crack, crack, crack, came a series of reports from aloft, and both men were settled, one spinning right across you – see, your coat is covered with blood. The explanation is that thirty feet up between the alleys of the trees floated the Attila, and Hartmann and Schwartz were indulging in a little sport. I very soon climbed up the ladder which was swinging close by the tree we were to have come to, and you were shortly afterwards hauled up in a carefully tied sheet. Why did we take you on board? I am surprised at your asking. We could not stop, and the idea of leaving you stunned, and in the compromising company of dead men, was not arguable. Would you have relished the idea of a trial as murderer and anarchist? You meant well, you see, by me, and the captain was strong in your favour. Some of the men know of you, and no one had a bad word to say – save that your theories were rather Utopian. But you may change."

For a while I was silent. I thought of my Utopian project. Then I said, "So far as my theories go, I will confine myself now to one remark. An airship may be used as well as abused."

Burnett laughed. "That's better! Don't forget, however, to define your view of us to the captain. Hallo! I must be off on watch!" An electric bell tinkled sharply in the outer chamber. "Good-night."

"Good-night."

Just before turning in I looked closely at the basin of my wash-stand. It was of the same silvery grey colour which I had noted on the walls of the cabin, and which, indeed, seemed ubiquitous. A sudden thought struck me. I emptied out the water and lifted it up. Its weight seemed so absurdly small that I could hardly believe my senses. But one thing was clear. The mystery of the thin silvery grey plate was explained. It was out of such materials that the body of the 'Attila' was fashioned. The riddle of Schwartz previously half brushed aside was at last solved completely.

As I was dropping off to sleep a novel reflection assailed me. What would Lena think of my absence tomorrow? Of this terrible night in the park she would not, of course, dream. Still...but sleep speedily quenched my thinking.

6. On the Deck of the Attila

It was late the next morning when thought and feeling came back to me, the blurred imagery of my dreams mingling strangely with the memories of the preceding night. Despite a slight headache, and a suspicion or two of giddiness, I felt as well as could be expected, and lying back snugly on my pillow began to meditate rising. For once my resolution was quick in the making. My uncle used to say that, all things considered, life was not worth the trouble of dressing. But on this particular morning it most certainly was. The apprehensions of the past night had given way to a hopeful spirit, while the interest of exploring this aëronef thrilled me through and through. I was about to spring out of the berth in readiness for the labours of the toilet when Burnett looked in through the door.

"All right? Glad to hear it. Where are we? Over the North Sea. Take my advice, and get up sharp. The captain has asked to see you. You'll find me knocking

71

about somewhere round here when you're ready."

Thoroughly alive to the situation, I was not long in getting into my clothes. But my disgust was great on feeling sundry half-dried splashes of blood on my coat, a souvenir of my luckless pursuer. In the excitement and darkness I had overlooked these hideous traces which now seemed to threaten me with the brand of Cain. Throwing aside the polluted garment, I stepped into the outer chamber, my pleasure quite overcast for the moment. Burnett was there, and a hearty breakfast was awaiting me, to which I promised to do summary and sweeping justice.

The room, but feebly apparent the foregoing night, was now flooded with the sunlight, but the height at which we floated rendered the air most chilly and penetrating. The silvery grey colour of the walls, floor, chairs, benches, tables, and even the dishes and mugs, wrought on me an impressive effect, curiously set off by the red cap worn by Burnett. Through the open doorway gleamed the same silvery grey livery of the flooring and bulwark of the passage already mentioned, and, framed, as it were, in silver, glowed a truly magnificent cloud-picture. This sky-scape, however, was unstable, mass after mass of mist, shaped into turrets, battlements, and mountains, rolled by in picturesque splendour, bearing artistic testimony to the speed at which we or they were moving.

"Beautiful, isn't it?" said Burnett. "Here, eat your breakfast, and then I'll show you round our cloud empire. Or perhaps you had best see the captain as soon as possible."

I said I thought that would be best.

"But where's your coat, man? Oh, I remember. Wait and I'll fetch you one of mine."

In a short time the missing garment was made good, and I was falling to with avidity.

"How do you manage your meals and service here? Have you cooks or servants?"

"Of course not. We are anarchists, and everything depends on private initiative. Every man is as good as another, and every man is a volunteer. Later on you will be expected to bestir yourself also."

"But how do you avoid chaos?"

"There is no chaos to avoid. Outside the engine-room and conning-tower there is little a man cannot quickly learn to do. We are very simple in our wants – that is part of our creed – and, consequently, have a deal of leisure. The watches are the worst part, for the captain is very particular."

"Ah, wait a minute. What authority has he?"

"The authority of the soul of this enterprise, and its best man. We would voluntarily support him in a crisis. Five days ago a couple of Italians turned rusty. He shot both where they stood, and the men in their hearts approved of it. But he is an iron man. Wait till you see him."

"Is any one on the Attila free to go where he likes?"

"Yes, except into the captain's quarters. To pass there a permit is required to all except myself, Schwartz, and Thomas. The engine-room watchers pass through every three hours, and a passage runs from it to the conning-tower and magazine below. You may guess what the latter contains."

"How many men are aboard?"

"Twenty-five, excluding ourselves. Eight are Germans, six Englishmen, four French, two Russians, one an Italian, and the others Swiss, some of those whom Hartmann employed at Berne."

"Berne; was that where the Attila was built?"

"That's it. Hartmann, Schwartz, and his Swiss workmen put her together. He made money there, as you know, and this was his grand investment. It was kept beautifully dark in the wooded grounds of his villa. We are going there now, so you will see the place for yourself."

"But does any one know of the Attila?"

"No outsider probably who would be believed if he said anything. We have our friends down below, of course – never you fear – but they are mum. The hour has not yet struck, but the preparations for the festival are being merrily carried out.

The Attila is a secret for the present. To avoid being seen we take every precaution possible, and never approach the ground except at night; in the daytime, well, there are clouds, and, if none, we simply mount higher, and then our colour is enough to conceal us."

"But what if you meet a balloon?"

"Oh, there's very little chance of that. And if there was, the balloonist might find cause to regret the meeting. But come, and I'll take you round to the captain. He is a better spokesman than I."

"Right you are."

We stepped out on to the passage, and rushing to the bulwark (if I may so call it) I gazed rapturously into the abyss below.

It was indeed a glorious sight. The clouds hung around and below us, but here and there through their rents flashed the blue of a waste of rolling waters. Ever and anon these gaps would be speckled with rushing sea-birds, whose cries, mellowed by the distance, broke on the ear like music. Above in the clear blue sky shone the sun at the keystone of his low winter arch, lighting up the cloud masses with a splendour words cannot describe. Far ahead through a break on my right a faint thin streak like distant land seemed visible.

"Hallo," I cried, "look there, land!"

Burnett shaded his eyes.

"I can see nothing. Ah, yes! By Jove! who's on watch? We ought to be rising."

As he spoke a sudden pitch of the aëronef nearly upset us – the speed rapidly increased, and the wind became positively cutting.

"We are rising fast," said Burnett. "See, we are leaving the cloud-bank far below us."

But a new marvel had just caught my eye, and, clinging to the hand-rail, I gazed upwards in astonishment. The wall of the chamber behind us was continuous with the main mass of the aëronef, which, looking from where we stood, exhibited the graceful lines of a ship's hull. Round this hull and presumably half-way up it ran the railed passage where we were standing, communicating here and there with doorways let into the grey side. Some thirty feet above us this side curved upwards and inwards so as to terminate in a flat, railed deck on which a few moving heads were just visible. But above this again rose a forest of thin grey poles running up to a vast oblong aëroplane which stretched some way beyond the hull. All these props were carefully stayed together, and those towards the bow were somewhat higher than those in the stern; provision being thus made for the inclination of the aëroplane consistently with due maintenance of the hull's equilibrium below. In the latter part of the nineteenth century much progress had been made in experiments with aëroplanes; those of Maxim being particularly suggestive and interesting. I was, therefore, at no loss to probe the significance of this portion of the mechanism.

"The captain wishes to see you," said Burnett, who was talking to a sullen-looking fellow by the doorway; "come along."

He stepped briskly along the passage, and, when we had gone some fifteen yards, turned up one of the alleys. Entering behind him I came to a small court surrounded with rooms and cabins, leaving which we ascended a spiral staircase to the upper deck. Glancing hastily around I saw five or six men pacing about chatting, while from other courts below came the sounds of singing and laughter. This deck, which capped the entire hull, was no less than eighty yards in length with an extreme breadth of at least thirty-five. Broad at the stern it narrowed off to a sharp point at the bow. The props attached to the aëroplane were set in six rows, curving close together amidships where there stood a small circular citadel, evidently the stronghold of the captain. Here were mounted three or four cannon of the quick-firing sort fashioned out of the same grey substance as the Attila, but the utility of which in a vessel carrying dynamite was not immediately obvious. The citadel itself bore no outward signs of comfort.

It had four square windows and a plain hole of an entrance let into bare shining walls. An exterior wall six feet high, surmounted with spikes, and having here and there a recess sheltering a machine gun, enclosed it. A fitter abode for the man I could not conceive. Sullen, isolated and menacing, it inspired me with a vague premonitory dread.

Burnett strode up to the entrance and pressed a knob. I heard the ting of an electric bell, and a man (Thomas, if I remember aright) came out and said the captain would see me alone. Mastering some natural excitement I bowed and followed him in. We passed through the inner portal and found ourselves in a narrow hall, flights of steps from which led down into the inmost vitals of the Attila. On our right was a door half open. My escort motioned me to enter and, pulling the door to, left me face to face with Hartmann.

7. The Captain of the Attila

Ten years had not rolled away for nothing; still the face which looked into mine vividly recalled my glimpse into the album in the little villa at Islington. Seated before a writing-desk, studded with knobs of electric bells and heaped with maps and instruments, sat a bushy-bearded man with a straight piercing gaze and a forehead physiognomists would have envied. There was the same independent look, the same cruel hardness that had stamped the mien of the youth, but the old impetuous air had given way to a cold inflexible sedateness, far more appropriate to the dread master of the Attila. As I advanced into the room, he rose, a grand specimen of manhood, standing full six feet three inches in his shoes. He shook hands more warmly than I had expected, and motioned me tacitly to a seat.

"You have heard about my mischance," I began tentatively. "I had hoped to meet you for an hour or so, but fear I have outstayed my welcome."

I felt he was weighing me in the balance.

"I know probably more of that mischance than you do. Those luckless detectives were certainly embarrassing, but, after all, they afforded us an incident. Of course, you can understand why we were bound not to leave you. And now that you are restored to vigour, are you sorry that you have seen the Attila?"

"On the contrary, I am lost in wonder. But look, sir, at the cost of my privilege. These unfortunate men you refer to, haunt me, and the purpose of this vessel, I must tell you, fairly appals me."

He listened approvingly. A man in his position can well afford to be tolerant.

"Oh, the men – such incidents must be looked for. Do generals dissolve into tears when two hostile sentries have to be shot? Do they shrink from the wholesale slaughter which every campaign entails? Nonsense, sir, nonsense!"

"But your war is not against this or that army or nation, but against civilization as a whole." I was determined to take the bull by the horns at the outset.

"You can scarcely justify that on those lines."

"Easily enough. The victory in view is the regeneration of man, the cost will be some thousands, perhaps hundreds of thousands or millions of lives, the assailants are our small but legitimate army. We can say that our friends below are sincerely devoted to us and to our objects; most of the ordinary soldiers of your princes have to be drummed into the ranks either by want or the law. As to the cost, look back on history. How many wars in those annals have been waged for the service of mankind? On how many massacres has one ray of utility shone? Now you must admit that our ideal is a worthy one even if unattainable. At the worst we can shed no more blood than did a Tamerlane or a Napoleon."

"Certainly the ideal is a grand one, and might, if reliable, be worth the outlay. But how many of your crew appreciate its beauty? Most, I will venture, love destruction for its own sake. Is Schwartz a reformer? Is Thomas?"

"My crew are enthusiasts, Mr. Stanley; nay, if you like, fiends of destruction. Every man is selected by myself. Every man is an outlaw from society, and most have shed blood. They burn to revenge on society the evils which they have received, or, given the appropriate occasion, would receive from it. In this way I secure resolute, fiery, and unflinching soldiers. But do not mistake my meaning. I know how to use these soldiers."

"I understand."

"Regard me according to Addison's simile, as the

angel who guides the whirlwind. Look on these men – well, as you will. They are like the creatures generated in decaying bodies. They are the maggots of civilization, the harvest of the dragons' teeth sown in past centuries, the Frankenstein's monsters of civilization which are born to hate their father. You have read Milton, of course. Do you recall the passage about Sin and the birth of Death who gnaws his wretched parent's vitals? It is the Sin of this industrial age which has bred the crew of this death-dealing Attila."

"But are all these men here morally rotten? The man Schwartz, they call your 'shadow,' is he a type?"

"Not at all. Your friend Burnett (who has just startled the Kensington Notables) seems sound. He is a madman of the more reputable sort. There is another like him with us, a German of the name of Brandt, a philosopher recruited from the ranks of the Berlin socialists."

"May I ask you two important questions?"

"Say on."

"The world says you were once a mere fanatical destroyer. Have you changed your creed?"

"You refer to my old days. Yes, you are right. I was then a pessimist, and despaired of everything around me."

"And you became an anarchist –"

"To revenge myself on the race which produced and then wearied me. I had no tutor but Schwartz, a faithful fellow, but a mere iconoclast. Our idea was simple enough. We were to raze, raze, raze, and let the future look to itself. Our mistake was in dreaming even of moderate success. Immunity from the police was impossible. But those wasted days are past."

He smiled ironically and bent his gaze on the wall, devouring, as it seemed, some specially pleasurable object. Following its direction, I became aware of a splendid sketch of the Attila, which constituted the sole æsthetic accompaniment of this singular sanctum. What a contrast it must have awakened between his present power and the abjectness of the fugitive of ten years back!

"One more question. How do you propose to conquer, now you have the Attila?"

"I cannot say much as yet. But, understand, the day when the first bomb falls will witness outbreaks in every great city in Europe. We have some 12,000 adherents in London, many more in Paris, Berlin, and elsewhere – they will stir the tumult below. London is my objective to start with. During the tempests of bombs, the anarchists below will fire the streets in all directions, rouse up the populace, and let loose pandemonium upon earth. In the confusion due to our attack, order and precautions will be impossible."

"You horrify me. And the object?"

"Is, as I repeat, to wreck civilization. If you are

83

interested, Brandt will probably attract you. He lectures to-morrow on the upper deck. We are Rousseaus who advocate a return to a simpler life."

"But how is the new order to take shape? How educe system from chaos?"

"We want no more 'systems,' or 'constitutions' – we shall have anarchy. Men will effect all by voluntary association, and abjure the foulness of the modern wage-slavery and city-mechanisms."

"But can you expect the more brutal classes to thrive under this system? Will they not rather degenerate into savagery?"

"You forget the Attila will still sail the breeze, and she will then have her fleet of consorts."

"What! you do not propose, then, to leave anarchy unseasoned?"

"Not at once – the transition would be far too severe. Some supervision must necessarily be exercised, but, as a rule, it will never be more than nominal."

"Your ideal, captain, amazes me. But the prospect, I admit, is splendid. Were you to succeed, I say at once that the return would well repay the outlay. I am a socialist, you know, but I have felt how selfishness and the risks of reaction hampered all our most promising plans. The egotism of democrats is voracious. It is the curse of our movement. But this scheme of supervised anarchy, well, in some ways it is magnificent – still it is only a theory."

"The Attila was once 'only a theory,'" rejoined Hartmann. "One word, now, Mr. Stanley. I ask you neither to join us nor to agree with us. You are your own master, and should you dislike this tour, say the word and at nightfall you shall be landed in France. If you elect to stay, well and good. I am your debtor. Don't look surprised, for you have been a good friend to my mother, and least of all men I forget debts. I only ask you to observe silence respecting our conversations, and never to interfere in anything you see in progress. Which is it to be?"

"I elect to stay. I can do no good by leaving, and by staying I court an absolutely unique experience. Believe me, too, captain, I am not insensible to what you have said. Between the anarchist Schwartz and yourself yawns an abyss."

"Good."

"One thing, captain. Could I find means to despatch a letter – a letter to a lady?" I added, as I saw his eyebrows rise slightly.

"Certainly, if you conform to the rules voluntarily agreed upon. You are not one of us – you will not, therefore, object to the letter being read. I will spare you undue annoyance by formally glancing over it."

"The rule is reasonable enough, captain, and requires no defence."

"It shall be given to one of the delegates when we touch land in Switzerland. A convention of importance is to be held there. But, come, I will take you round the Attila," and striding by me he passed out of the study.

"What was that land visible just now, captain?" I asked, as we reached one of the stairways that led down into the vessel.

"Holland. The course has since been altered; we find the clouds are lifting, and not wishing to run too high are making off towards the English Channel. Tonight we shall cross France, steering above Havre along the channel of the Seine, over Paris, Dijon, the Saone, and the Jura mountains into Switzerland. I had intended to go to Berne, but have been forced to change my plans. We shall stop over a forest not far from Lake Leman, where some fifty delegates will meet us. After that we return to London."

"For war?"

"For war."

Down into the depths of the Attila we went, the spiral stair running down a deep and seemingly interminable well. On reaching the bottom my conductor turned off into a passage brightly lit up with the electric light. A rumble and thud of machinery broke on the ear, and in a few seconds we stood in the engine-room of the Attila. My readers are aware of the wonderful advances in electricity made in the early part of the twentieth century, and I need not, therefore, recapitulate them here. In the mechanism of this engine-room there was nothing specially peculiar, but the appropriation of the best modern inventions left nothing to be desired. Electricity, according to the newly introduced method, being generated directly from coal, the force at the disposal of the aëronaut was colossal, and, what was even more expedient, obtained for a trifling outlay of fuel. A short but very thick shaft, revolving with great speed, led, I was told, to a screw without, and by the sides of this monster two others of far humbler dimensions were resting idly on their rollers.

I was now able to solve the riddle of the Attila's flight. The buoyancy of the vessel was that of an inclined plane driven rapidly through the air by a screw, a device first prominently brought into notice by the nineteenth-century experiments of Maxim. The Attila, albeit light, was, of course, under normal conditions, greatly heavier than the quantity of air she displaced – indispensable condition, indeed, of any real mastery over the subtle element she dwelt in. The balloon is a mere toy at the mercy of the gale and its gas – the Attila seemed wholly indifferent to both.

But, desirous of probing the problem to the bottom, I put Hartmann the question –

"What would happen supposing the shaft broke, or the machinery somehow got out of order?"

"Well, we should fall."

"Fall?"

"Yes, but very gradually at first, so long as our speed was fairly well maintained. The aëroplane, as you know, will only buoy us up on the condition that we move, and that pretty quickly. Still, there are always the two spare steering screws to fall back upon."

"But what if they stopped as well?"

"It's most unlikely that they would stop. The three shafts are worked independently. But if they did, the sand-valves would have to be opened."

"The sand-valves?"

"Yes. You have doubtless been surprised at the huge size of the Attila. Well the main parts of the upper and middle portions of her hull are nothing more nor less than a succession of gas-meters – of compartments filled with hydrogen introduced at a high temperature, so as to yield the maximum amount of buoyancy. Below these compartments again lie the sand reservoirs. When these latter are three parts full their natural effect is to keep the Attila at about the level of the sea, supposing, that is to say, the screws are completely stopped. If your so-much-dreaded event was to happen, the watch in the conning-tower would simply shift the sand-levers, a quantity of ballast would be released, and we should at once begin to rise. We can thus regulate our weight at will. The secret of it all is the marvellous lightness of these walls. I am not free to tell you to what discovery that lightness is due, but you may test and analyze as much as you like, on the off chance of a correct guess."

"It's all superb!" was my enthusiastic comment. "But how about an ordinary complete descent to earth?"

"A very simple matter. From the outer gallery the Attila looks as if her bottom was gently curved, terminating in the customary orthodox keel. That is what the upper lines suggest. But three feet below the level at which we stand lies a flat projecting bottom studded underneath with springs resting on the axles of wheels. I wish to touch land. I press certain knobs and this, that, perhaps all three screws, ease off, run down, or may be reversed. The Attila then sweeps onward much after the fashion of an albatross with outspread motionless wings. Steering is easy — a 'ting' in the engine-room sets this or that side screw shaft rotating. Slowly — perhaps fast — she falls, then faster and faster. Meanwhile I stand by the sand-levers — I pull this and the stern rises, we swoop down like a hawk; I pull that, the bow rises, the impetus thus gained carries the Attila in a noble curve aloft.

Finally she hovers over the ground, and, opening a hydrogen valve, I adjust her descent delicately, so as to spare the springs."

"But you must lose a great deal of hydrogen in this manner."

"Not so much as you would think. And, besides, the loss if of no moment. We carry an immense quantity of the gas compressed in tubes at a pressure of many thousand pounds to the square inch. What loss there is can therefore always be made good at intervals. You will have a chance of watching our procedure very shortly, as we 'sand up' and replenish three or four gas-reservoirs at a sand-dune not very far distant."

We passed through the gaily-lit passage back to the well, where for fifty feet above us the long stair curled upward to the citadel.

"These side walls," observed Hartmann, "with those constituting the outer skin of the Attila, bound the huge gas compartments I mentioned. They are independent, so that serious accidents are impossible. In the cavities and corridors between them lie the cabins and quarters of the crew, the courts enclosed by which you must have noticed from the upper deck. All these courts open on to the outer gallery, and communicate by the deck with the common room. To the centre divisions of the ship, the engine-room, and the conning-tower, no one has access except with my leave. This –" and he opened a small carefully guarded door, "– is the magazine."

He pressed a button, and the gleam of a vacuum lamp pierced the darkness. Half awestruck I stepped within.

"There is nothing to see now. We have to be so cautious. Stay! look here." He seized a ring and lifted a trap in the floor. I started back, for it opened into a well some three feet deep and then into the aërial abyss below!

"That well will vomit disaster one day."

He let down the trap, and we left the gloomy chamber.

"The Attila, you see, Mr. Stanley, combines the advantages of the bird and the balloon, of the aëronef and the aërostat. It has been my dream from boyhood, and at last, after infinite pains, it is realized. Still, even for me it is but a means to an end. But you will admit it is not a bad one."

We ascended the stairway and stepped on to the upper deck. Some twenty men were assembled, and they respectfully saluted my companion.

"Comrades," he said, "my friend Stanley comes among you. Though he is not yet one of us, he may be. His devotion to the cause of Labour is his passport. Take him and treat him as our guest."

He bowed to me and retired into his citadel.

The crew crowded eagerly round me with a warmth wholly unlooked for. The terrible captain had evidently not spoken in vain. During the next half-hour I was escorted round their quarters in state. Naturally I volunteered my services for the necessary work of the vessel, but somewhat to my surprise was firmly asked to desist. A guest, they said, could not be expected to conform to their habits at once, and two of the objectors were urgent in entreating me to accept their services. In the end I was vanquished, not entirely to my regret, and the first day of my sojourn on the Attila passed pleasantly enough. Would that all the others had passed in a like manner, for in that case I should have to describe an Elysium instead of an Inferno!

8. A Strange Voyage

Released for the moment from care, I gave myself up to the full enjoyment of the voyage. Of the grandeur of the cloud pictures, the glory of the sunsets and the twilights, of the moonlight flooding our decks as we sped over the streaky mists below, of the mystic passage by night and the blushes of early morn, I cannot trust myself to speak. Such things ordinarily belittle words, but framed in the romance of this voyage they wrought indescribable effects upon me. The economist was merged in the artist, I no longer reasoned but lay bathed in the flood of feeling. And not only these beauties enthralled me, but the motion of the Attila was itself a poem.

Have you never in the drowsy noon of a long summer's day lain back on the sward watching the evolutions of a rook round its elm, noted the rapturous poise of its wings and the easy grace of its flight? Even such was the flight of the Attila. Let me detail an incident which took place overnight, and the ground for my enthusiasm will be obvious. Hartmann had summoned me to his study, and taken me along to the conning-tower, the passage to which ran under deck from the citadel. The tower (capped with search-light apparatus for night work when requisite) rested on the nozzle or ram-like projecting bow of the aëronef, and was so constructed as to command a superb outlook. Two men were on watch when we arrived, and these respectfully saluted the captain.

"Is the shore far off?"

"About five miles."

"Any vessels in sight?"

"No, sir."

"All right."

"Now, Mr. Stanley," said he, turning to me, "I am going to show you how the Attila obeys its master. We require to load up with sand and refill five or six or the hydrogen compartments. That strip yonder is one of our favourite docks. Watch me."

He pressed one of the knobs communicating with the engine-room.

"That stops the force supply to the main shaft, the revolutions of which will speedily ease down. We are falling fast, do you observe? Hold tight. There!"

The bow dipped several degrees and we shot onward and downward like an arrow. Were we rushing into the sea, the billows of which seemed to leap up at us larger and larger each second? Another pitch, the bow rose considerably, and we were carried by the aëroplane hundreds of yards upwards, the onward motion being at the same time inconceivably rapid. Once more these tactics were repeated, and so closely we neared the ocean that the waves must have splashed the screw-blades. Meantime Hartmann rapidly twisted a wheel with each hand.

"This works the sand levers of the bow, that of the stern. Ballast is dropping quickly."

At once we rose, and to my unconcealed wonder stopped at a height of about 300 feet above sea-level, still, however, riding forward with a lazy careless motion. We were now near the sand-pits, whither a few turns of the screw bore us gently. Hartmann, watching his opportunity, began twisting a small wheel in the centre of a medley of others.

"A hydrogen valve."

We fell sharply, but a touch to the other wheels eased us, and alighting gently on the spit the wheels of the Attila were buried up to their naves.

It was then getting late, so every one was as expeditious as possible. First bag after bag of sand was dried and cast into the sand reservoirs, binding the craft immovably to the dune. The process resembled a coaling operation at Port Saïd, and amused me greatly. I worked hard, and carried a shower of praises. Afterwards I stood by while the five huge centre compartments were filled with the rarefied gas. It was a tedious affair, because each in turn had to be pumped and re-pumped out, then filled with cold hydrogen, then with a fresh supply highly heated so as to contract and become rare on cooling. About one hour was consumed in the operation, and at its close the Attila still lay motionless on the sand-spit. Everything, however, having been duly overhauled, the sand levers were gently worked, the surplus ballast slipped away, and breaking away from our couch we floated twenty feet above the spit. The three screws were then set rotating, and speed having been attained, we curved upwards into the bosom of the sunset clouds. An experience more superb romance itself could not furnish.

Later on we passed at high speed over Havre, the lights of which twinkled merrily through a mist patch. Next Rouen glided away beneath us, and at seven we swept over the gorgeous city of Paris. Satiated in some measure with these sights I stepped down into a court and entered the cosy smoking-room. Burnett was there, and Brandt, the 'philosopher' whom Hartmann had mentioned. I was very fond of German thought, and did not fail to improve the timely occasion. Brandt was not only a metaphysician, but readily listened to my very guarded criticisms of the anarchists. He was, however, inflexible, and professed the most supreme confidence in Hartmann. "He is the heart of the enterprise, and it was he who gave the Attila wings. Look at what he effected with small resources, and you may rely on him with great." He evinced a sturdy faith in the scheme of supervision, and prophesied as its result a grand moral and intellectual regeneration of man. But, he added, the initial blows will be terrible. One remark filled me with apprehension. "London," he said, "in three days will be mere shambles with the roof ablaze."

"Heavens!" I cried, "so soon!"

"Yes. The object of this trip is merely to settle details with some terrestrial friends who meet us tomorrow evening – delegates from the various affiliated bodies of Europe."

Shortly afterwards I had an interview with Hartmann, and urged that some warning might at least be given to our friends.

"By all means," he remarked, "warn yours to keep away from London. One of the delegates will act for you after the inspection of the message. For myself, I have already taken my private precautions."

DIARY. Tuesday (Morning). – Crossed Dijon and the river Saone in the night. Rising rapidly, as the slopes of the Jura mountains are ahead of us, and 'the captain,' as they call him, will insist on keeping high! No doubt it is safer, but I suspect the real truth is that he wants to appear unannounced over London – a portent as mysterious as terrible. Shows himself ironical and inflexible. I suggest a mild course of action, and he asks me whether I aspire to be captain of the Attila. Am becoming nevertheless almost inured to the thought of the impending calamity. Brandt says philosophically that 'the advance of man is always over thorns.' Unhappily the thorns do not always lead to happiness. Will they do so in this case? The bluster of the vulgar dynamitards is revolting. Even Burnett is forgetting the end in the means. As to Schwartz, his vile parody is being sung freely by all the English-speaking hyænas of his stamp:–

The dynamite falls on castle walls,
And splendid buildings old in story.
The column shakes, the tyrant quakes,
And the wild wreckage leaps in glory.
Throw, comrades, throw;
Set the wild echoes flying;
Throw, comrades; answer, wretches,
Dying, dying, dying.

Am getting to loathe the crew, now the novelty of their reception is beginning to wear off.

Tuesday (Afternoon). – Still higher, great discomfort being experienced. The barometer readings make us three and a half miles above sea-level over the pine-covered summits of the Jura mountains. I find it necessary to breathe much more rapidly, the rarity of the air is unsatisfying. At times a dizziness seizes me, and on examining my hands and body I find my veins standing out like whipcord. Hartmann shortly eases off the screws – he was experimenting, so it appears, with his machinery. A change of tactics is observable. He ignores possible sightseers now, probably because he knows that reports from tourists and mountaineers stand no chance of being believed. Hence we almost brush the mountains, and a superb privilege it is. The magnificent pines here surpass anything else of the kind. Sometimes we glide mid-way along a valley with a rushing torrent beneath us and these pine-fringed precipices on our sides; sometimes we amaze a luckless mountaineer or shepherd as we thread a defile; sometimes we curve over valley-heads with a grace an eagle might imitate; then, again, we breast the cloud-rack and are lost in its mantling fleeces. We are now bearing south-east by south, and are not far off from the beautiful lake of Geneva.

Tuesday (Night). – Wrote my letter and telegram, and gave them to Hartmann for the delegate. We have stopped over a pine forest some five miles distant from Morges, on the shore of the lake. Switzerland, I am told, was selected as the rendezvous because of its central position. Many Russians, Poles, Austrians, and Italians, besides delegates from other nationalities, are expected. They are to arrange details of the forthcoming revolution. Had a friendly talk with Burnett, who once more tried to proselytize me. Told him if any one could shake my convictions it is Hartmann and not he. How bloodthirsty the men are getting! Query. – What if the lust for blood grows by what it feeds on? What if this crew gets out of hand? Happily, a strong man stands at the helm.

(Later). – The convention is in full swing. What enthusiasm must inspire these 'tourists', for, of course, it is in this character that they travel. Most, I hear, are very badly off, their funds being supplied by their associations. A great deal of provisions and matériel has been brought aboard. How well this crusade is organized!

Hartmann remains on board, he has never left the vessel except on the occasion when he visited his mother. Burnett and Schwartz take his instructions to the delegates, and most of the crew escort them. We are floating very near the ground in a rude clearing on the mountain side, two rope-ladders and some cables link us with the soil. After several hours' conference below, the delegates visit the Attila. Heavens! what desperadoes some look! Yet they control, so Burnett says, vast societies. Hartmann interviews each. He works patiently through the list, and finally addresses them en masse, launching terms of the most animated invective against modern civilization. Am, of course, excluded, but learn that everything has gone off admirably. Five of the delegates are to join the crew, the rest carry back their instructions. We start early in the morning. What a spectacle there is before us! However, two days' breathing time is something. Trust that delegate, whoever he is, will not forget the telegram and letter to Lena.

9. In at the Death

During the return to England two incidents of note, both alike terrible, but terrible in widely different ways, chequered our voyage, and the first of these it will now be my task to detail.

Wealth of romance, witchery of mountain scenery, and panoramas of ever-varying landscapes in the plains – whatever happiness can be gleaned from these was mine in bounteous plenty. Hitherto, however, the Attila had met with gentle winds and fairly clear skies; she was a gay butterfly by day and a listless moth by night. She had shortly to display to me her prowess as a rider of the tempest. This experience, along with its sequel of grim incident, impressed me deeply. I shall try to awake in the reader some echo of the emotions which it stirred into fervour within me.

No one, at any rate, could charge Hartmann with boring his unsolicited guest. Feasted as I had been with pictures, I was destined to be swept through ever novel galleries of natural marvels. I had anticipated that we should return by a like route to that by which we had arrived, but a pleasant reversal of this view was in store for me. Leaving the slopes of the Jura behind her, the Attila sped in a south-westerly direction across the department of Aisne, over Lyons, westward across the extinct volcanoes of Auvergne, then curving slightly to the south she leapt the river Dordogne, and, finally, passing at a great height over Bordeaux, reached the ocean rim over the desolate Landes which span the coast-line betwixt the Garonne estuary and the Adour. Had I been exploring Central Africa in the interests of science, I should feel justified in presenting my observations at length. But the tracts beneath me being so familiar, such procedure would be both useless and troublesome. I must therefore leave the imaginative to put themselves in my place and picture these well-known districts as transfigured by the romance of air-travelling.

In looking down on such natural maps one is transported with a sense of power and exultation that renders even homely sights attractive. Burnett, it is true, assured me that even this luxury of travel palls on one after a time. Judging from the indifference of the crew, I should say that he had right on his side. But, whether my artistic appetite was abnormal, or the banquet provided was not of the proper duration,

I can only say that this part of my residence on the Attila always wore the livery of a gorgeous dream.

It was becoming dark when the pine forests and sand wastes of the Landes gave place to the rim of Biscay surf. In accordance with custom we rapidly began to descend, and were soon coursing over the billows at a height of some 200 feet. It was one of those evenings which ordinarily favour melancholy and lassitude. Above us stretched inky layers of stratus or 'fall' cloud, wrought of mists driven from the upper regions by the chills that hurried after the setting sun. The wind blew in gusts and preyed vampire-like on our energies – an electric tension of the atmosphere was becoming unmistakably manifest. Clouds were rising smoke-like from the ocean rim and mingling with the flatter masses overhead, and even as I gazed the waves seemed to flash whiter and whiter through the veil of the nether darkness.

I was standing on the upper deck debating social problems with Brandt, greatly to the enjoyment of three of the crew who watched the contest. Some few yards in front of us the platform tapered off to a point at the convergence of the bow railings, and directly in front of this the hull sloped downwards and outwards to form the projecting ram. At the extremity of this, with crest barely visible from the spot where my listeners were reclining, rose the conning-tower like a horn on the snout of a rhinoceros. Amidships and astern hummed the forest of stays and props which hung us to the aëroplane, clustering thick over the rounded boss of the citadel, now half shrouded in gloom. It was a scene to inspire the painter – this weird vessel and its weird crew borne along between an angry welkin and the riotous surges of the ocean.

"Violent diseases often demand violent remedies," said Brandt, as he developed his favourite topic. "The surgeon may be gentle at heart, but he spares not the gangrenous limb. In modern times he has anæsthetics to soothe his patient, but did he shrink from his task when such artifices as these were unknown? Regard us anarchists as excising the foul ulcers of Humanity and as forced to perform that duty with no anæsthetics to aid us. Could we throw all London, all Paris, all Berlin into a trance, how painless would be our surgery? But, unhappily, we have to confront struggling patients vividly sensitive to the knife. Nevertheless, for their own sakes, or rather the sake of Humanity, we must cut."

"But you overlook one important contrast. The surgeon lops off a limb or roots up an ulcer to save his patient's life or better his health. But you attack civilization not to reform it but to annihilate it."

"That is true, but civilization – your industrial civilization – what is it? Not a system to be identified with the cause of human welfare, and hence worth preserving in some form or other at all costs, but a mere vicious outgrowth prejudicial to that welfare as we conceive it. The test of the worth of a civilization is its power to minister to human happiness. Judged by this standard your civilization has proved a failure. Mankind rushed to her embraces in hope, fought its way thither through long and weary centuries, and has for a reward the sneers of a mistress as exacting as she is icy: '*The third day comes a frost, a killing frost.*'"

During the delivery of this harangue the wind had been steadily rising, and it now began to shriek through the stays in a fashion positively alarming. Foregoing further parley, I bent over the railing and strove to catch a glimpse of the angry sea-horses beneath us. But it was by this time too dark for the non-feline eye. Glancing upwards and around the horizon, I could see the awnings of the storm unrolling, with here and there a rift through which stole the feeble moonlight. A man came from the citadel and stepped up to us. It was Hartmann.

"Well," he said, "we are in for it. The barometer is falling rapidly, and the storm is already gathering. Have a care for yourselves, comrades," he added to his followers. "You, Stanley, follow me to the conning-tower. The log of the Attila may be worth writing tonight."

I followed him gladly into the citadel, and down the stair leading to the narrow corridor which ran on to the bow. As we entered it the Attila seemed to reel with a violent shock that sent me spinning against the wall. The storm had burst. By the time I had picked myself up Hartmann had disappeared. I found my way after him into the tower, where he was standing, regulator in hand, with his eyes on the glass plate that looked forward into the night.

"We are rising," he said, laconically. "Look!"

A fan of vivid glory cleft the darkness. Illumined by the electric search-light great masses of driving vapour were rushing by us; but other sight there was none. Suddenly a second squall struck us, and the Attila rolled like a liner in a cyclone; the lurch was horrible, and for a moment I thought we were capsizing – it must have been one of at least forty-five degrees followed by a very slow recovery. Hartmann was busy over a medley of wheels, levers, and regulators.

"We are passing through the cloud-belt at a very high speed," he continued, as if the shock was a trifle. "My intention is, first, to let you see a storm from the quiet zone above it; secondly, to rush downwards into it that the Attila may show her mettle."

I said nothing, for my feelings were in truth somewhat mixed. With the ascent portion of the programme I concurred heartily; the second I would gladly have abandoned, as it seemed to me so utterly foolhardy. But faint heart was not the commodity for Hartmann, and wishing to earn his favour through his respect, I suppressed my fears resolutely. Not noticing my silence he kept on throwing in his comments on the situation. As the minute wore on I observed that the mist masses were blowing thinner and thinner against the bow of the Attila. Suddenly the electric light was turned off, and a gentle silvery glow took its place. And as we swept on I perceived that the wind had fallen also. Hartmann pressed a bell-knob, and the two men on watch reappeared.

"Now to the deck again, and you shall see a fine picture."

As we stepped into the court of the citadel I had reason to appreciate this remark. Down in the conning-tower I had stood behind the captain and seen little save the dawn of a gentle radiance among the thinning mists. But up here the vista was glorious. A brisk but by no means stinging wind swept the deck. Above shone the horned moon in unclouded majesty, casting a weird light on the rolling masses of cloud-battalions underneath us. From below came the roar of the strife of elements and the crooked gleam of the Levin-bolt, while the echoes of the thunder leapt grimly across the halls and palaces of the storm-king. As if arbiter of the struggle, the Attila rode serenely over the turmoil in the quiet zone.

"How high are we now?" I asked Hartmann, for the air was oppressively rare.

"A trifle over two miles. A sublime spectacle this, is it not?"

"Uniquely so. The sense of serene power is so striking. But you do not propose to rest here?"

"Oh no. I must show that this serene power is not fraudulent. I shall shortly plunge the Attila into the very vortex of the storm, and teach you how nobly she can wing her way through it."

"It would not be safe, I suppose, on deck, what with the rolling, pitching, and wind? Still one can scarcely enjoy these scenes in the conning-tower, where the engineer and watchman usurp the best places."

"You would like, if possible, to stay here?"

"Yes." If the experience had to be undergone, there was no reason why I should not brave it out thoroughly. Better the deck than a back seat in the conning-tower.

"Well, so let it be. But you must be lashed securely. Where shall it be? Why not to the railing over the bow? You could not have a finer coigne of vantage."

I assented at once, and, a couple of the crew being hailed, I was speedily made fast in a sitting posture by the waist and liberally invested with wraps. My position was excellent. I could see down the sloping bow to the conning-tower, and would be fairly sheltered from the worst of the wind. All the preparations being complete, the captain and the crew retired, leaving the deck altogether deserted. No light, save that of the moon, fell on its cold surface, and that only where the umbrella-like aëroplane did not bar off the sheets of slanting silver.

The Attila rode grandly over the gloomy woolpacks below, and, thrilling with excitement and some fear, I waited for the coming plunge. The suspense was short. Suddenly the electric eye of the aëronef glowed forth from the crest of the conning-tower, behind and above which I was lashed to the railing. Then the bow dipped and the speed began to increase. Again and again it dipped with a series of little jolts, and then cut obliquely into the tenuous rim of the cloud-belt, through which it began to plough with an energy almost distressing.

Those who have stood on an express engine running sixty miles an hour will know what it is to breathe in the teeth of a rushing blast; let them then conceive my experience when 120 and probably more miles an hour were being done in a hurricane. Drenching clouds swept over me, the wind and thunder roared round me, as I was borne into that angry stratum below. Burying my mouth within my neckcloth, and sheltering my eyes with my hands, I looked straight ahead at the glow which cleft the darkness before us. In a very brief time we had shot through the belt, and were rushing wildly down to the wind-lashed desolation below. The pitching and rolling of the aëronef now became terrible, and once more awoke my fears. What if the guns were to break adrift or the props of the aëroplane to yield! As it was I could see that the squalls caused a startling irregularity of course, the Attila swerving furiously from right to left, now dropping like a stone, now being checked in her descent and hurtled upwards. Surely Hartmann would not run too close to the waves on such a fearful night!

Looking downwards, I now saw that the glow had reached the face of the waters, everywhere in violent turmoil with huge waves at least twenty-five feet high from trough to crest, spanned by clouds of wind-drift. And a sight still more enthralling was a large dismantled steamer labouring heavily as she lay hove-to under the strokes of a thousand hammers. With boats smashed, bridge carried away, bulwarks in many places shattered, and decks continually swept, she was a spectacle fit to move even a Hartmann.

Assistance, however, was out of the question. Every art of the captain must be required to guide the course of the Attila, and our tremendous speed could not safely be relaxed for a moment. It would have been, indeed, easy to 'hover' in the teeth of a furious blast, but what if the blast were to drop and leave us

momentarily stationary, while a side roll or pitch were to succeed? Screws and sand levers notwithstanding, it was better to risk nothing. But what an experience was this! The Attila with flaming electric eye circled round the doomed vessel, lighting up a deck crowded with panic-stricken passengers, groups of whom every larger wave washed pell-mell through the broken bulwarks. Cry or shriek, none could be heard, the roar of the elements was too frightful, but the gestures of the wretches were too piteous to misinterpret. Shutting my eyes, I refused for some minutes to look on the dreadful holocaust, but once more I had to yield to the fascination. By that time the drama was over. The Attila was still circling, but in the place of the luckless vessel leapt the white-maned savage billows.

I now began to feel chilled and miserable; the excitement of the outset had dwindled, and a reaction, enhanced by the rigours of the night and the foregoing drama, mastered me. Happily the Attila had by this time weathered enough of difficulties. Rising through the cloud-belt, she left the angry winds and rain once more below her. Some of the crew ascended to the deck and released me from my bondage.

It was now getting late, so after thanking Hartmann for his courtesy, I descended into my berth to sleep off the ill effects of exposure, and dream horrible dreams of wrecks and drowning victims.

10. The First Blow

I rose late the next morning somewhat the worse for my exposure, but nevertheless far too interested in my voyage to heed a mere cold and a few rheumatic twinges. No sooner, indeed, was I awake than I leapt out of my berth, and busying myself energetically with my toilet, was speedily pacing the bulwarked passage of which mention has already been made. The zone through which we were ploughing was cloudy, and a strong bitter head wind was blowing. Looking over the bulwarks I could see nothing but driving mists, and above the vast aëroplane a thinner layer of mist, through several rifts in which the sun thrust his slanting columns of light. No one was visible in the passage, but I heard a medley of excited voices which suggested that some controversy was in progress on the upper deck.

Listening attentively, I became convinced that some unusual affair was in hand, and anxious to miss nothing of interest, I entered an arch that led into one of the courts, and passed up the enclosed spiral staircase to the scene of this animated talking. On gaining the deck I saw nearly all the crew standing in groups round the citadel. Burnett was there gesticulating wildly to Brandt, so stepping briskly up to them I asked the cause of this muster.

"Ah, you here!" said Burnett. "In time for the first blow, eh! Well, there will be something to see shortly, eh, Brandt!" and the anarchist-philosopher addressed smiled approvingly. But his merriment recalled the bland purring of a cat over a captured mouse.

"What's up, then?" I continued, somewhat startled, for during the pause the ominous words "ironclad," "bombs," uttered by some of the eager disputants around, had caught my ear.

"The captain has sighted an ironclad, and we are about to try conclusions," said Brandt. The words had scarcely passed his lips when the inner door of the citadel swung ajar, and through the enclosure into our midst stalked the redoubtable captain himself.

"Comrades," he said, "below us steams a large British ironclad just sighted through the mist. I propose to test her mettle – it will serve as a practical test of our bomb-fire – are you agreeable?"

A burst of applause greeted this iniquitous

proposal, and a sturdy rascal stepped out of the throng and saluted him. Hartmann bent forward. "Well, Norman," he said.

"May I strike the first blow, captain?" A chorus of similar applications followed. Hartmann thus suggested that the applicants should draw lots for the privilege, and the ruffians proceeded forthwith to settle their claims in this fashion.

Their levity so disgusted me that I longed to rush forward and attack the whole scheme. I had actually moved forward some steps when I felt a tight grip on my arm. I turned round sharply, to face Brandt, who had providentially sensed my project.

"Back, man! Are you mad? These men will stand no nonsense, and if you insult the captain, even his personal influence could not save you."

Bah! it was hopeless. I slunk back with a feeling of utter helplessness. There was clearly nothing for it but to see the whole hideous affair out in silence. Still, indignation all but mastered me. What ruffians were these anarchists! "Cowards!" I hissed involuntarily, but by this time they were too absorbed in their lot-drawing to hear me. "Shut up, fool," reiterated Brandt. "I warn you that you will be brained or chucked overboard if they hear you." I bit my lips in despair. "Schwartz has it! Schwartz has it!" I heard Hartmann say at last – they were drawing the lots – "he strikes the first blow, and no better man could do it. Next, Norman; next..."

I walked away and leant on the bow railing, glad to be left alone. The hubbub continued for some time, when the men dispersed, almost all going below. Torn by useless emotions I gazed down at the mists that swam beneath us, striving to pierce the veil which separated us from the doomed ship. To tear myself away from the spot was impossible – the fascination of the projected crime was irresistible. Have you ever watched a scene in a slaughter-house, loathing it while nevertheless unable to avert your gaze? Possibly you have. Well, that situation is akin to the morbid curiosity which nailed me unwillingly to my post.

The mists were thinning around us, but I observed with some surprise that a dense cloud below us – cut off sharply from its now unsubstantial fellows – maintained its position relative to the Attila unchanged. Evidently Hartmann was purposely lurking behind this barrier, and proposed to deliver his first blow on an absolutely unsuspecting victim. Looking more attentively I noted a thin longitudinal rift in this cloud through which could be seen, though dimly, the sea, and in this something dark and indistinct, no bigger than an ordinary pea. It was the ironclad!

The Attila began to sink rapidly – the rift lengthened and broadened as I gazed, the pea swelled into a two-masted, two-funnelled battle-ship with a trail of black smoke faintly decipherable in her wake. Down, down, down we dropped – we were now on the fringe of the upper surface of the cloud, and the great ship, now only some 300 feet below us, was revealing itself clearly to the eye. At this point our downward motion ceased, and the Attila began to describe short curves at the level of the screening cloud, now skimming over its dank masses, now flashing over the rift that stretched directly over her unsuspecting prey. Four evolutions of this sort had taken place, and now for the fifth time we were gliding over the rift, when I heard a cheer raised by some men on the lower gallery, and craning my head over the railing, saw something black flash through space and splash in a big green wave that was flinging itself against the vessel's stern. It was the moment of the "first blow," and – might the omen hold good! – the first blow had failed.

Again a curve over the rift, and once more a failure, at least so it seemed at first, for this time, again, a splash by the stern rejoiced me. But my satisfaction was momentary. A few seconds after I saw a cloud of smoke shoot upwards from the ironclad, followed by a deafening crash. The third bomb had told. And in the horrid confusion that followed, the Attila threw off her secrecy, slipped through the cloud, and floated down to the vessel like some huge bird of prey – the very embodiment of masterful and shameless power.

As the smoke cleared away, revealing the strange visitor from the clouds, the feelings of the officers and crew must have been as unique as they were terrible. Amazement, a sense of complete unpreparedness and helplessness, going along with the disastrous results of the explosion, must have unnerved even the boldest. The great battle-ship was wholly at the mercy of the foe that rode so contemptuously above it.

How the situation was viewed from its decks has been told at length in the admirably graphic letter of Captain Boyes, R.N., to the Times, and to that source I must refer you for details. Looking down from my eyrie, I was of course only able to gauge very roughly the havoc wrought by the bomb. Hartmann had previously told me that nothing constructed by man could withstand his enormous missiles, and the scene below well bore out his boast. Apparently the bomb had burst amidships nearly, I should say, between the funnels. Of these latter one had been shorn of half its length, the other had been blown away completely, its base forming part of a chasm whence rolled volumes of black smoke, through which the shrieks of wounded men rose faintly upward. Across this chasm had fallen the fore-mast, while fragments of spars, ventilators, steel plates, fittings, boats, and human victims were scattered confusedly over the low-lying fore-deck. And even as I looked two more appalling explosions shook the ironclad from stem to stern; through the uprush of smoke I saw a great telescope of a gun tossed out of its shattered turret into the water and a huge cantle of the steel deck torn away, as if it were paper, exposing a new chasm, at once invaded by flames. But the other bomb was even more deadly, bursting in the great hollow excavated between the funnels and wrecking the very vitals of the ironclad; the steam from the shattered boilers rushing tumultuously up the gap with the effect of speedily shrouding the whole vessel. Some horrible deaths, says Captain Boyes, sprang from this explosion, as all those on duty in the port stoke-hole and engine-room were either blown to pieces by the bomb or subsequently boiled alive. I did not, of course, know of this at the time, but the volumes of escaping steam told too clearly how hideous must be the massacre, and imagination thus stimulated could not very well go far wrong. I felt giddy with horror when I thought of the scenes which that vapour-pall hung over.

How long was this drama to continue? Doubtless until the ironclad was gutted or sunk, a consummation which could not be very far distant. Two or three bombs more would surely complete the work, and leave perhaps no witness to tell the hideous tale to history. I could look no longer – to do so seemed almost abetting these cruel fanatics – but flinging myself on the deck awaited tremblingly the next burst of thunder. A minute ebbed away, another, and then another, and still no shock. The suspense was becoming acute.

Suddenly the Attila pitched violently, the bow shifting thrice vehemently upwards, and along with this the hum of the great screw-blades began to swell higher and higher. I sprang to my feet – these tactics meant, of course, a rapid ascent, but what was the object in view? Glancing over the railing I perceived that we were slanting at great speed into the cloud-zone, leaving the crippled battle-ship far behind and below. Ah, yes! The reason was clear enough. Not a mile to the south-west a large ironclad attended by some smaller vessels, probably cruisers, was making its way to the scene. Owing to my absorption in the attack they had hitherto escaped my notice.

"A poor job this," said some one who had stolen up unperceived behind me. I turned round – it was Burnett.

"Very," I answered. "I must congratulate you, I suppose, on the heroism you have just displayed. A pity not to enhance it by engaging this vessel's consorts."

Burnett took the sneer coolly.

"Why waste material? Besides, you must see

that the Attila would be uselessly exposing herself. It would be folly to risk the salute of heavy guns with the great campaign yet before us."

He was wise after his kind. The Attila dared not face the newcomers, who by elevating their guns might well succeed in winging her. A shell from a five-ton gun would have proved a most damaging visitor. Only so long as she circled directly above a vessel could she count on immunity from serious injury. A contest at her old level with numerous scattered foes was impracticable; so huge a target would inevitably be holed in the long run, while an attempt to drop bombs from a higher level would defeat its object by rendering accuracy of aim impracticable. Perforce, then, she had dropped the prey from her talons and was seeking safety aloft. Mounting into cloud-land, she was departing as mysteriously as she had come, a tigress who, having once tasted blood, yearned to slake her thirst in the heart of civilization itself. Tomorrow we were to reach the metropolis, and then – sick with my forebodings and savage at my sense of impotence, I turned surlily away from Burnett, whose very presence was now becoming obnoxious, and descending into a court passed thence through the gallery to my berth and resolved from that hour to see as little of my fell associates as the conditions of my stay rendered possible.

11. A Tempest of Dynamite

On the morning of October 19th, that most memorable of days in the history of revolution, we sighted Brighton through the haze, and secrecy being no longer observed, the Attila swept down like an albatross into the sight of men. Gliding two hundred feet above the water she presented a truly majestic spectacle. The vast sweep of her aëroplane, the huge size of her silvery grey hull, the play of the three great screws humming with the speed of their rotation, the red-capped aëronauts lining the upper deck and lower gallery, the nozzle horned with its quaint conning-tower, and the four ominous cannon leaning downwards from the citadel, these and the marvellous flight itself commanded the homage that hailed her. The esplanade and the beach buzzed with wonder beneath us, and as we skimmed over the housetops beyond them streets seemed to fill as if by magic.

Thunders of applause rose behind us as awe regularly gave place to admiration. "They will sound a different note tonight," said Schwartz, who was standing by me. "The banquet at last is ready, and surely we shall eat till we are gorged."

The Attila gradually rose higher, as the slopes of the South Downs confronted her. But she always kept about one hundred and fifty feet from the ground, deliberately courting the observation which she had once so shunned. Of her purpose or ownership no sign however was given; it was pleasant to play with the unsuspicious fools whose lives and possessions she had so ruthlessly marked for her own. A more fascinating sight than this journey it is not easy to picture. Now, for the first time in my life, I fairly revelled in the incense of my fellow-creatures' astonishment. To dance butterfly-like over woods, fields, hills, and sinuous rivers, to grasp vast ever-changing vistas of scenery, are in themselves delicious. But when to these purely artistic joys are added those of power, when the roar of wondering cities rises upwards, and you lean over the bulwarks serenely conscious of superiority, you must be described as realizing here on earth one of the paradises of dreamland.

At about ten o'clock we passed over Grinstead, and shortly afterwards crossed the boundaries of Sussex. By this time the preparations on the aëronef were complete, and every one had been summoned to the citadel and sent to his post. And now there fell upon me the shadow of the coming disaster. The faces of the crew were savage, even Brandt had lost his kindliness. Burnett was surly, and asked how I liked my position. Rather nettled, I told him that at any rate my hands would be free from bloodstains. Then it occurred to me that I might glean some interesting news from Hartmann.

Eager for some excitement, as the depression stole heavier and heavier upon me, I ascended to the upper deck and pressed the button by the gate of the sombre citadel. Thomas appeared and telephoned my request to see the captain. The reply came back that he was in the conning-tower, but would be glad to see me for a moment. Accordingly, I was not long in making my way along the passage that led from the citadel to that favoured spot.

"Well," he said, "I trust your nerves are in order. The drama opens in an hour. Within three days' time London will be in ruins, and 'Lord Macaulay's New Zealander' will be able to commence his survey."

"Is there no way of avoiding it? In the name of humanity, captain, I beseech you to pause. Think of the agonies which this awful resolve must breed! Think..."

"No more of this," he said sharply. "You are my guest. You may, if you wish, be landed. You may, if you wish, remain. But in the latter case you will conform to my ruling."

"And that is?"

"That you hold your tongue when desired to. London, I say, as Cato said of Carthage, London must be destroyed."

"You have the advantage, captain. But thank heaven this will be no catastrophe of my making. And now may I ask a rather leading question?"

"By all means. At the worst you can only be refused an answer."

"When and how will the first blow be struck?"

"Above the Houses of Parliament; a blank discharge of the cannon will warn all, after which my flag will be run out. And then…well…"

I understood.

"We shall conduct the attack in three ways – by shell firing and machine-gun fire, by dynamite and forcite bombs, and by streams of burning petroleum."

"Good God!"

"Meanwhile our associates will be spreading devastation below. The Houses of Parliament, the City,. and the West End will occupy us in turn."

"Who will control operations?"

"Schwartz, Norris, and Brandt manage the bombs. Five Swiss, the oil; the rest – with the exception of three in the engine-room – man the quick-firing and machine-guns. I myself shall direct the course of the Attila from this tower. You are free to walk the upper deck, but the lower gallery is being transformed into tanks to hold the oil. I must now ask you to go. Thomas, you will see Mr. Stanley on to the deck and place him under due watch. He is free to inspect all he wishes, but he must interfere with nothing – understand, with nothing either by word or deed. Any breach of the order will entail death."

I was as helpless as a bluebottle in a spider's web. Thank heavens that I had sent Lena that telegram and letter. Luckily, in any case, she and her parents ought to receive warning from the guarded hints doubtless already conveyed to Mrs. Hartmann.

When I reached the deck, Thomas (who acted as a sort of aide-de-camp) ordered a man to watch me, and then sped away below. Looking over the rail, I could see that the oil was being poured into tanks formed by fitting cross walls into parts of the lower gallery. There were some eight of these along the bow end of the vessel alone, and I trembled to think of the fearful mischief which these hideous contrivances portended. Lamentations of this sort were, however, futile. Casting an eye over the landscape, I saw Caterham vanishing beneath us, while to the right rolled the billowy expanse of the North Downs. We were now going at a high speed, and in a short time

– far too short to my thinking – were rapidly skimming over Croydon, Norwood Junction, and the Crystal Palace. We were now nearing our destination, and our altitude, recently raised to one of five hundred and fifty feet above sea-level, was once again suddenly altered to one of one hundred and fifty. The speed, too, was rapidly reduced, till at last gliding gracefully over Lambeth we passed obliquely over Westminster Bridge.

The scene here beggars description. The enormous crowd, already massed for some great labour demonstration, usurped every available patch of standing room, windows and roofs became animated, and vehicles of all sorts and conditions pulled up in batches and served as the vantage-ground of excited groups. Probably the arrival at Brighton had been at once telegraphed to the newspaper offices, but few knew of it, and to those few (the anarchist 'brothers' apart) the Attila was necessarily a complete mystery. To the majority we came as falls a bolt from the blue (I refer here to the universal astonishment apparent, for at the outset it was clear enough that the aëronef inspired no terror). Cheers shook the air beneath us, and the distant thunders of applause rumbled far away down the Embankment.

A man stepped aside from his gun, and pointed down at the crowd on Westminster Bridge.

"This is the bridge blown up by Hartmann and Schwartz ten years ago. These vermin seem to have liked it, don't they?"

I turned away in disgust. What a mockery it was! The populace thought they were applauding an inventor, and they cheered a ruthless destroyer! Terrible captain, *Morituri te salutant.* But the hour had come, – the clock-tower rose only twenty yards from us.

Suddenly a gong sounded ominously. It was the signal. The four quick-firing guns vomited flame simultaneously, and ere the crash had died away, a blood-red flag was to be seen fluttering at the stern. The crew yelled with excitement, as well they might, for the coup was evilly romantic. On its broad fluttering bosom the flag bore five ominous words – words which carried a terrible commentary with them –

THUS RETURNS HARTMANN THE ANARCHIST.

It was a shock never to be forgotten. The cheering ceased in an instant, and in its place curses and howls rose up from the struggling mob. Even the sightseers on the roofs shook their fists at the Attila.

"Ah, vermin!" yelled one of the crew, "you will howl louder soon."

The words had scarcely left his lips when the Attila was sharply propelled onwards, the force being such as to cause me to grasp the railing to save myself from falling.

The object of this manœuvre was evident. It was necessary to rise, now that we were recognized, and active operations were to commence. After a series of brilliant wheels the Attila climbed high above the clock-tower and commenced to cruise about in large circles.

The gong sounded once more. Once more the quick-firing guns vomited flame, and this time the charge was not blank. And mingling with their almost continuous roar, there now came a crash of appalling magnitude, shaking the very recesses of one's brain. Another and another followed, till the air seemed to beat in waves upon us, and our ears became veritable torture-chambers. Then followed a rattle like that of a landslip. I looked over, to start back with a shriek. Horror of horrors, the great tower had fallen on the crowd, bruising into jelly a legion of buried wretches, and beating into ruins the whole mass of buildings opposite. Every outlet from the neighbourhood was being furiously fought for, hordes of screaming, shrieking madmen were falling, crushing and stamping their victims into heaps, and with the growth of each writhing heap the ghastly confusion grew also. Of the Houses of Parliament pinnacles were collapsing and walls were being riven asunder as the shells burst within them.

But this spectacle, grievous of its kind, was as nothing to the other.

With eyes riveted now to the massacre, I saw frantic women trodden down by men; huge clearings made by the shells and instantly filled up; house-fronts crushing horses and vehicles as they fell; fires bursting out on all sides, to devour what they listed, and terrified police struggling wildly and helplessly in the heart of the press. The roar of the guns was continuous, and every missile found its billet. Was I in Pandemonium? I saw Burnett, black with grime, hounding his comrades on to the slaughter. I heard the roar of Schwartz's bombs, and the roar of the burning and falling houses. Huge circles of flame raved beneath us, and shot up their feverish and scorching breath. The Attila, drunk with slaughter, was careering in continually fresh tracts, spreading havoc and desolation everywhere. To compare her to a wolf in a flock of helpless sheep is idle – the sheep could at least butt, the victims below could not approach, and after some time, indeed, owing to the smoke, could not even see us.

The morning passed in horror, but the story of the afternoon and evening is wilder yet. The sky, overcast with clouds and black with uprolling smoke-wreaths, lay like a strangely spotted pall over the blazing district. Around and within Westminster enmity could do no more. Shortly before two o'clock the Attila drew off. With the screws working powerfully she climbed upwards into the heavens, and buried in the cloud-masses gave London a momentary respite. Hartmann wished not to fatigue the crew, being anxious to reserve their energies for the attack on the City. His aim was to pierce the ventricle of the heart of civilization, that heart which pumps the blood of capital everywhere, through the arteries of Russia, of Australia, of India, just as through the capillaries of fur companies in North America, planting enterprises in Ecuador, and trading steamers on African rivers. 'Paralyze this heart,' he has said, "and you paralyze credit and the mechanism of finance almost universally." The result already known to history proved too well that he was right; but my task is not to play the historian, but simply to tell my tale as one who has trod the Attila.

The interval of respite was not long, but during the whole time we kept well veiled within the angry zone of clouds. Burnett came up to speak to me, but I received him coldly enough. Schwartz was 'surprised that I had no compliment' for him when 'even the captain' was pleased. He remarked that the slaughter had been prodigious, that the Houses of Parliament were wrecked, and the flames were carrying everything before them. Nero fiddling over Rome was respectable compared with this monster; but to attack him would have been fatal, as I should have at once been shot or thrown overboard. Hartmann remained invisible, he was still at his post in the conning-tower.

Towards three o'clock I noticed the men hurrying hastily to their posts. The assault was shortly to begin.

Slowly we emerged from the cloud-rack, wheeling over in great circles above the luckless quarry below. A queer accident delayed us. I was standing by the citadel when I heard a sharp crack, followed by a sensation of rapid sinking. The shaft of the main screw had broken, and we were rushing downwards like a parachute. Everything for the moment was in confusion and more than one cheek paled, but a master-hand was in the conning-tower. Without even handling the sand levers, Hartmann set the auxiliary screws rotating at a high speed. At once the fall was checked, and the Attila rose once more into the clouds.

After an hour's delay the shaft was temporarily repaired, and arrangements were made to replace it, if necessary, with a spare one. Luckily for the aëronef these shafts were extremely short, so that two spare ones could always be kept in hand without undue demand for stowage room. The present mishap was not at all serious, as between the repaired shaft and the spare ones there was little, if anything, to choose. The only 'lucky' thing was that the snap had not taken place too close to the stern. In this case the screw-blades might have torn away the stern-plating and irretrievably damaged themselves at the same time.

The Attila now began to re-descend, working

all three screws at once. We were evidently not
unexpected, for I made out soldiery in the streets, and
several detachments of artillery. How they expected
to wing us I really do not know, for a moving aëronef
hurling forcite and dynamite missiles is neither an easy
nor a pleasant target. The height at which we were
must also be borne in mind. I suppose I am within
the mark when I say that our descent stopped at the
half-mile limit. There was no delay this time. The first
and second bombs fell on the Tower, reducing it half
to ruins; they were of the largest kind, and terribly
effective instruments. Meanwhile the quick-firing guns
played havoc at all points of the compass. But the
worst was to come. As we rode over the heart of
the City – that sanctum of capital, where the Bank of
England, many other banks of scarcely less brilliant
fame, the Royal Exchange, Stock Exchange, with credit
companies, insurance offices, and discount houses
innumerable lie herded – the bombs fell in a tempest,
shattering fabric after fabric, and uprooting their very
foundations. There was a constant roar of explosions,
and the loss of life must have been something terrible.
Burnett was in his element. Handling his gun like a
practised marksman, he riddled St. Paul's and its
neighbourhood, the crash of the infalling dome rising
even above the explosions around it. But for him, at
least, there was retribution. Hitherto, bating rifle-fire,

we had escaped being hit as the motion and height of the Attila were in our favour. South London enjoyed the downfall of the shells launched against us. But, as fate would have it, a volley of grape-shot struck us. From the sides of the aëronef they rebounded, steel armour would have been more easily pierced, but a stray one found a billet. Burnett was gazing over the side through the smoke at the wreckage when a ball holed his throat. He fell back with a gurgle. I rang up, and saw the man was failing – the blood was spurting from his carotid like jets from a siphon. In less than a minute he was dead.

His fate was deserved, and I felt no ray of sympathy, for by this time I was dead to all feelings except those of helpless hatred for the anarchists, and horror at the hideous slaughter below. Before this horror every former sympathy with Hartmann and his crew had withered. Could I have killed Hartmann at that moment I would gladly have paid the price for it. But his day of reckoning was to come.

12. How I Left the Attila

The death of Burnett drove the crew to frenzy, their curses were not those of men but of fiends. The shock of surprise – the fury that one blow of their despised victims should have told – goaded them into the mood of Molochs. Instantly the news flew to Hartmann, who returned a welcome answer. The yells around me were broken by a burst of laughter.

"What is it?" I asked, fearful of some new horror, full as the measure of crime now seemed.

"Wait and you will see!" was all the reply I got.

The Attila began to move at a high speed, and four of the men rushed down on to the lower deck. Quicker! quicker! quicker! – there was no doubt of it, we were swooping on the City like a falcon. I was at the rail in a moment, and, careless of uprushing shot and shell, bent over the side in a fever. Though beyond the zone of flames, a Simoom blast swept the vessel, and puffs of inky smoke spangled with sparks rendered breathing a torment. But the Attila swerved not an iota. Down we swept like a hurricane over the yelling maddened throngs massed in Farringdon Street. Suddenly I heard a sharp cry:

"Stand off!" I had hardly time to draw back when a column of flames shot up the side, reddening the very bar I had been clutching.

"Let go!" – a crash, the column vanished, and a stream of fire like a comet's tail drew out instantaneously in the wake of the Attila. It was the petroleum. The first tank had been lighted, its contents shot over the shrieking wretches below! For full fifty to sixty yards the blaze filled the roadway, and the mob, lapped in flame, were writhing and wrestling within it. A fiendish revenge was glutted. Suddenly I was hurled violently to the deck as the bow rose sharply. The Attila, buoyed by her aëroplane, shot once more aslant to her old higher level, firing her guns continuously as she ascended. Sick and surfeited with horror I remained lying some time where I was. But the end was yet to come.

By this time the night was pressing on rapidly, but what a night! I rose up and staggered to the stern – anything to be away from these wretches. The hum of the great screw-blades reached me, and I looked over and yearned that they might fail us. We were now circling over Fleet Street and the neighbourhood of the Strand. The fires lighted at Westminster in the morning

were carrying all before them, and a crimson yellow rim stretched all the way from Whitehall to Victoria. On our flank the City was blazing, and a roaring tumult of flames was undulating in every direction from this centre. And now for the first time I saw that others than ourselves were hurrying on the incendiary work below. There were visible blazing circles in South London over the water, blazing circles far away in North London, and blazing circles scattered throughout the West End. The delegates had kept their faith. The great metropolis seemed doomed. I shuddered to think what the mob might do in their despair. The West End was even now probably being looted, and the worst passions would toll its death-knell. I thought of my telegram, and found some relief in the belief that Lena at least was out of danger.

Suddenly I shook with terror. I had never asked Hartmann whether the letter and the telegram form had been handed to the delegate. Racing back to the citadel, I appealed to one of my guards. Could a message be sent to the captain? Certainly. The reply came back in about ten minutes. It was to the effect that they had been handed to Burnett for one of the French delegates. Had Burnett, then, given them? It was just possible that he had not. Kneeling by the body I ransacked the dead man's pockets. My worst fears were realized. In the breast-pocket of his coat lay the precious and forgotten missives! My heart seemed to stop for the moment, and then beat with hammer strokes. I made a desperate resolution. I must see Hartmann at all costs, and wring from him the permit and opportunity to descend. Doubtless it was entering the shambles of a desperate city, now being wrecked and pillaged by its own inhabitants; it was entering the lion's den possibly only to find a victim before becoming one myself; but whatever risks I ran, honour scoffed at delay, and love winged me with ardour.

"Tell the captain I must see him. Tell him the letter was never delivered, and that I must somehow find a means of speaking to him face to face." The answer came that he could not possibly see me, and that I must say through the telephone what I wanted, and that briefly. I shouted that I must at all costs descend. He replied that his plans were unalterable. I entreated, I clamoured, I expostulated, pleading the friendship I had borne to his mother, and the possibility that she, too, had not yet stirred. His words to her had necessarily been more or less enigmatical. Let me, then, go and watch over the fate of her also. I had moved him, for there was a long pause. After what seemed ages of waiting came his reply. "The Attila cannot descend, but it crosses Hyde Park shortly. If the case is urgent, take my parachute. The fall will not be of more than five or six hundred feet."

This alternative was gruesome, but there was no help for it. I wavered an instant and accepted. Shortly afterwards Norris appeared on deck, and bade me follow him into the citadel. I entered it, crouching low down to the deck with the fire of the guns darting forth above me, and down the steep stair we went till we reached the door of the dynamite room. My guide pushed the door open and we entered.

A solitary electric lamp dispelled the gloom of the chamber and revealed the figures of Schwartz and two other men standing by the trap-hole, now for the moment closed. I was struck with the caution with which their work, judging from appearances, was done. From a cabinet in the right-hand corner sloped a stoutly-made tube of network, well stayed by bands and roping to the ceiling. It was evidently along this that the dangerous bombs were guided, rolling into a bag-like compartment immediately over the trap. I had scarcely entered when the trap was lifted, the compartment lowered, its terrible passenger released, and the bag sharply pulled in. To forego a glance was impossible. I leant over the aperture and listened for the voice of the fatal messenger. It exploded near Oxford Street below us, apparently in a house, for the secondary rattle was tremendous, suggesting the crash of ruined walls on the roadway. Schwartz was about to launch another when a ting of the call-bell arrested him.

He telephoned to Hartmann, and received the order to cease dropping bombs for the present. The reason was simple enough, they were about to utilize a new weapon, the petroleum, which up to this time had done duty only on the hideous occasion already mentioned.

Norris now stepped up to Schwartz and told him of my determination. The German's wicked eyes twinkled.

"Good. I, too, descend to-morrow, and we may meet."

"Better luck," I said bitterly; "I have done with the Attila for ever."

"So, ah! you Socialists have much to learn. Well, we are teaching you something in London."

I managed to keep my temper, for these were not men to be played with. But how I would have liked to have hurled the miscreant down that trap-hole.

Norris muttered that the mob might teach me something too, and I realized, then, that the descent was not my greatest danger.

What if the parachute were to be seen by any one? I should be torn to pieces or worse. The possibility was an appalling one. Still the darkness would prove a very serviceable shield. Once clear of the Park, I could pilot myself through the streets without trouble.

"Here, the captain sent you this revolver. You may need it to defend yourself, not that I care a cent. And now look sharp, we are coming over Park Lane in a minute."

Norris pointed to the trap-hole, and I saw swinging at the side a long rope-ladder.

"What, climb down that?"

"Yes, if you want to go. There's no other take-off good enough. Come, yes or no, we shall be spinning across the Park before you've done thinking."

"But the parachute?"

"There it is in the corner. It is a case of clinging on with your hands. We will lower it to you, and at the word 'Go,' drop it. The only risk is trees and the cursed vermin underneath. Will you go?"

There was no help for it. I clenched my teeth savagely, and backed kneeling on to the edge of the trap-hole, grasping the bomb-tube with my left hand to steady myself. Schwartz and another man got ready the parachute and thrust its stem down the opening. It was lucky the Attila did not pitch, for these tactics might have proved my death-warrant. As it was, I succeeded in working my toes into the top, and thence into the lower rungs of the ladder. Having thus worked my way down I looked for the parachute, and transferred my left hand from the tube to the trap-edge. Slowly I climbed down; the oscillations of the ladder were startling, and feeling for the rungs was a purgatory. At last I was clear of the well, and under the bottom of the aëronef hanging in a clear space between the huge wheels which studded it. "Now's your time!"

yelled Norris, and I grabbed the rope-handles of the parachute fiercely – now with my right hand, then, as the ladder threatened to run away from under me, with my left. One look below – we were full over the Park, five hundred feet or so from the turf.

"Let go!" I shouted, and flung my legs from the ladder on which they were resting obliquely. For a second and a half my heart seemed to leap into my mouth, for I fell as falls a spent rocket. Then with a welcome tug on me, the parachute bellied out, and fear gave place to confidence, nay, to exhilaration.

What a spectacle! Above me fled the Attila like some evil bird of night; north, west, south, east rose the crimson hues of the smoke-wreaths; below I heard the clamours of the populace, and saw the darker tree-tops stand out against the dark face of the Park. The wind blowing strongly I was borne south near a patch of trees, and had reason to fear for the moment that a nasty mishap was imminent. Happily fortune favoured me, and gliding oilily and without shock to the ground, I made off rapidly in the direction of Bayswater.

13. In the Streets of the Burning City

Thus far I had fared unexpectedly well. By the luckiest of chances I had alighted without having been observed, and this was the more remarkable seeing that the Park swarmed with noisy multitudes which I could not have sighted from the trap-hole. Not thirty yards from my landing-place some brawl or outrage was in progress, and the deep curses of men mingled with the shrieks and appeals of women told me that it was no mild one. As I neared the Bayswater Road, I came upon crowds of fugitives from the fire, and the almost equally cruel mob, now master of the streets. Delicate ladies and children, invalids shivering in their wraps, aristocrats, plutocrats, and tradespeople were huddled into groups of the oddest imaginable composition. Many of the men carried weapons, and it was well for them and their convoys when they did so, for bands of ruffians were prowling round robbing, insulting, and murdering at random.

One savage brute rushed at me, but a seasonable click of my revolver sufficed to sober him. All this time I was being devoured by anxiety. The terrible licence here boded no good for Carshalton Terrace, always supposing the Northertons had received no benefit from the guarded hints given to Mrs. Hartmann. Bearing in mind my interview with the old lady, I had grave cause to fear that these hints had been far too vaguely worded, in which case nothing was more likely than that they had been ignored. Who, unless clearly warned, would have looked for a revolution so sudden and mysterious as this? Hartmann had wished to spare his mother new revelations during his short visit, but he had of course wished also to warn her of these impending horrors. He might have well fallen between two stools, and robbed his well-meant caution of the emphasis and impressiveness it called for. The upshot of the night proved that my fears were only too well founded.

A bright light shot downwards from the sky on a patch of buildings which were immediately lapped in flames. I understood; the drama was running into its third act; the Attila, then soaring some two miles away over Kensington, had exchanged the rôle of dynamitard for that of an aërial pétroleuse. A more frightful conception had surely never entered the mind of man. All the more reason for despatch in case things had gone wrong at the Terrace. Hurriedly fighting my way out of the Park, I joined the tumultuous yelling mob that flowed like a river in flood along the Bayswater Road in the direction of Notting Hill. But what a gauntlet I had to run! The mansions lining the thoroughfare were being looted by the dozen and their inmates shamefully maltreated or butchered, while in many places the hand of the incendiary was crowning the work of destruction. It was opposite these last-mentioned places that the struggles of the mob were most arduous. After a house had been alight for some time, the passage past it necessarily became dangerous, but owing to the steady pressure of the mass of people from behind, no one once entangled in the mob could hope to avoid it. Numberless deaths occurred by the mere forcing of the fringe of the crowd on to the red-hot pavements, and into the yellow and ruddy mouths of the outleaping jets of flame, and these deaths were terrible sights to witness.

For myself I had seen from the first that the press could no more be stemmed by me than rapids can be stemmed by a cork. One could get into the stream easily enough, but getting free of it was quite out of the question. It was a case of navigating between Scylla and Charybdis. On the one side I saw men and women crushed, trampled on, and suffocated against the railings. On the other I saw scores forced into the flames which their own comrades had kindled. The safest place was in the current that was now sweeping me along, a current which ran some three feet off the pavement on the left, a place fairly out of reach of the flames and blasts of heat from the houses on the opposite side. By dint of great efforts I managed to keep in this, though strong cross-currents often threatened my safety, and at last, sorely bruised and battered, with face scarlet with the scorching heat, found myself opposite the Queen's Road. Here I seized my opportunity and, working clear of the stream, dodged in among a thinner crowd, wearied, but still intent on my purpose.

As I rushed in and out of the groups and files of self-absorbed people, I became aware that I should speedily be left almost alone. Thinner and thinner grew the groups, and the reason was easy to discover. Right ahead of me, from the Queen's Road Station downwards to Westbourne Grove, the streets on both sides were being fired by bands of red-capped ruffians followed by armed companies of marauders with their vilest passions unchained. Not a soldier, volunteer, or policeman was visible – the whole organisation of society seemed to have fallen through. Ever and anon sharp revolver cracks and rifle reports testified to hideous scenes in these houses, and women, chased by flames, or even more cruel men, could be seen to rush shrieking into the street. I knew how severe a gauntlet had to be run, but, clutching my revolver, made a dash along the centre of the roadway. As I passed a shop vomiting clouds of smoke and sparks, a miserable woman rushed out and clung to my knees in a frenzy, entreating me for the love of heaven to save her. Even as she clung to me two of the red-caps dashed after in hot pursuit, but I lost no energy in parley. In less time than it takes to write of it, I shot them down, and leaving them bleeding and dying, dragged my charge into the centre of the roadway.

"I can't stay!" I shouted. "Work your way up the street into the crowd going to Shepherd's Bush. It's far safer there." Then, without waiting for a word, I plunged once more down the street – between the fiery houses glowing like coal under forced draught – between the incendiaries, the butchers, and looters – over smoking stone-heaps and rafters – till with singed clothes and almost stifled with smoke I found myself in Westbourne Grove. Here I saw a terrified horse lying between the poles of a splintered cart. I was going to shoot him out of mercy, when the thought struck me that he might be useful. Hastily loosening the harness, I assisted the poor beast to rise, and leaping on his back galloped down the Grove Road. The windfall was indeed propitious. Within ten minutes I found myself on the pavement by Carshalton Terrace, where, tethering my steed to the area railings,

I leaped up the steps to the door. Thank goodness! the district as yet was unharmed. Furiously I plied the knocker, beating the panels at the same time with my revolver-butt. Then I heard old Northerton shout angrily through the letter-slot, "Who's there?"

"Stanley, Arthur Stanley," I answered deliriously, and the door instantly opened. One warm shake of the hands – "And your wife and Lena?"

"My wife is inside, but we are in a fever about the child. She has not returned, though she went out early this morning."

"Where, where?" I clamoured excitedly. "D'you know the streets are shambles?"

"My God! yes; but where she has gone we can't tell. Her maid heard her say that she went to see an old lady in Islington, but nothing…"

"What! Islington! Are you sure of this?"

"Yes, why?"

"Because I know the place. Now, cheer up. There's no call for panic; I'll start at once. – No, I must run the gauntlet alone – horse outside waiting – no good burdening him with two riders."

"Godspeed."

I was out of the hall in a moment, and in another had untethered and sprung upon the horse. A wave of the hand to Northerton, and the road began to rush away under me.

14. A Nocturnal Ride

Of the details of this ride I need hardly speak. Anxious to avoid the rioters, I steered my course by as northerly a curve as was practicable. The street lamps were, of course, unlighted, but the glow of innumerable fires reflected from every window, and beaten downwards by the crimson clouds overhead, was now turning night into day. As I galloped through the streets of Marylebone, I caught a glimpse of the Attila wheeling far away over what seemed to be Kensington. But of the few awkward incidents I can scarcely now remember one; my chief enemy indeed was a poignant anxiety about Lena.

It must have been ten o'clock by the time I galloped into Islington, tired, hungry, and unkempt, but devoured by emotions which sternly forbade a halt.

Five minutes brought me to the villa, and throwing the reins over the railing, I pushed the gate aside and entered. The door of the house was open, and the sound of voices came from within. Revolver in hand I entered, but a glance dispelled my apprehensions. The little room so familiar to me was full of terrified women, with here and there a sturdy workman among them. At my entrance there was something like a panic, but I speedily reassured the company.

"Where are Miss Northerton and the old lady?" was my first question after soothing the tumult. A sister of charity came forward.

"Upstairs. Do you bring any message? Mrs. Hartmann, I must tell you, is dying."

"But Miss –?"

"Is safe and in attendance upon her."

A wave of delight rolled through me. How selfish we all are! The news about Mrs. Hartmann weighed as nothing with me for the minute.

"Can I send a message to the young lady?"

"Is it important?"

"Very."

"Then I will take it myself."

I scribbled a few words on a scrap of paper and handed it to the sister, who immediately left the room. I had not long to wait before she returned, saying that the lady would see me upstairs.

I was shown up to the sick-room, where Lena was sitting by the bedside. She greeted me with a regard chastened by the gravity of the occasion. After a moment's delay, I stepped up to the bed and looked at the patient. She had been unconscious, so they told me, for some time, and was now dying rapidly. A few hurried whispered words told the story. Mrs. Hartmann had gone to Westminster with Lena on the fatal morning of the previous day, to witness the great labour demonstration, and the old lady had been brutally trampled in Parliament Street by the mob. Indeed, but for a company of volunteers who succeeded in momentarily beating back the rush, both ladies would have perished, said the sister. Mrs. Hartmann, thus barely snatched from death, had felt well enough to struggle back to Islington with Lena, having, after an hour of weary waiting, and at great expense, procured a cart and driver. Everything seemed on the high-road to chaos, and the return was only accomplished after great risks had been run from the mob. Things looked better, however, when they managed to get out of the more central districts, and ultimately they reached the villa in safety, considerably surprised at the relatively quiet state of the neighbourhood. Soon after entering the house, however, Mrs. Hartmann was attacked by violent pains and nausea, and on the advent of a friendly doctor it was found that she had sustained the most grave internal injuries. Hæmorrhage set in later, and she rapidly became worse.

Before becoming unconscious she had dictated a letter for her son (nobody knew that he was alive, added my informant), and had desired Lena to hand it to me for transmission. Very pathetic in character, it narrated the facts here recorded, and ended with 'a last appeal' to him from a 'dying mother' to better his dark and misguided life.

Poor lady, she little knew who her son really was, and how he had himself unwittingly hurried her to the grave.

Mrs. Hartmann passed away about an hour later. Lena and I reverently kissed the aged and venerable forehead, and paid the last tributes to our friend. Then leaving the death-chamber, I took Lena into a morning room and acquainted her with my extraordinary experiences since we had parted. She listened with the keenest interest, and was appalled to think that Hartmann – the anarchist assailant of London – could be the son of the poor harmless lady whose body lay so still in the adjoining chamber. Sometimes indeed she seemed quite unable to follow me, and bent searching glances on me as if to make sure that I was not after all romancing. No doubt my tale sounded fantastic; but conceive the man who could 'romance' on so peculiarly solemn an occasion!

"But did you not see the aëronef yourself?" I asked.

"No, we were hopelessly jammed up in the crowd

near Whitehall. The wildest rumours were afloat, fires were breaking out everywhere, cannon booming, and the mob breaking into shops and stores. It was impossible to see far owing to the smoke."

A bright trail of light flashed down the heavens to the south-west.

"Look, Lena! look! there is the Attila itself! Now will you believe me?" The deluge of fire had not yet ceased to fall! We stood riveted with horror to the window.

"Do you see the search-light glowing on her bow – the blazing petroleum splashing down from her sides on to the house-tops? Ah! there will be a pretty story to tell of this in the morning."

Lena could only gasp in answer. The Attila with her one electric eye stood out sharply against the crimson-hued clouds, with trails of fire lengthening out behind her. And as the burning liquid fell, one could see the flames from the gutted houses leap upwards as if to greet it. Whole acres of buildings were ablaze, and one dared not think what that deluge must mean for the desperate mobs below. And no human art could avail here. In this extraordinary vessel the vices and powers of man had been brought to a common focus. The Attila seemed mad with the irresponsibility of strength and yet to the captain of that fell craft, now suspended in mid-air over the doomed city,

I had somehow to transmit the letter of his dead mother. The thought struck us both at once.

"What about that letter?" said Lena, as we watched the destructive gyrations of the aëronef. I took it from her hand reverentially.

"I shall do my best to deliver it. One of the crew" (I remembered Schwartz' remark) "is likely to descend shortly. Possibly I may meet him. If not, I must wait for my chance. Believe me, Lena, this letter, if I can ever deliver it, will prove the most terrible retribution possible. And now we must be off; your parents are seriously alarmed, and for their sakes you must ride back with me without delay.

It was late in the morning when I snatched a broken rest at the Northertons'. But in seeking my sofa – it was far too terrible a time to think of bed – I had at least the consolation that Lena was restored safe and sound to her father and mother, and last, and perhaps not least, to myself. It seemed, too, that we could detect some lull in the fury of the conflagration, though to what this was due we were unable, of course, to ascertain. Lull, however, or no lull, caution was still indispensable, and old Northerton and the butler, armed to the teeth, kept a dreary vigil till the morning broke in sullenness.

15. The Morrow of the Disasters

It was late when I came down-stairs to learn what the night had brought forth. Mrs. Northerton was kindness itself, and persisted in regarding me as Lena's heroic rescuer, whereas I had really done nothing which entitled me to distinction. Our midnight ride had been only that of two people on one horse, for no molestation whatever had been offered us. Still, taking time by the forelock, I suggested that the rescuer had some claim on the lady, and, finally, revealed our secret at the true psychological moment. Mrs. Northerton said she had long looked forward to the union, and that her husband had been quite as sagacious as herself. She was only sorry that things looked so black around us. How would all this anarchy end? It was scarcely a time to think of Hymen. For aught we could tell we might all be beggared, or possibly even butchered, to make an anarchist's holiday.

The story of my adventures was retold in detail, and the astonishment of my hearers at the revelations knew no bounds. They had wondered greatly at my absence, but were now of opinion that to have sailed the air in the Attila was a privilege the historian would grudge me. I replied that the spectacle of the great massacre was so far from being a privilege, that the bare memory of it horrified me. Had I known exactly what to expect, I should have accepted Hartmann's offer and have been promptly landed beforehand.

My narrative having come to an end, we were speculating on the outlook, when a tramp of feet arrested us, and all four of us rushed simultaneously to the window. Good cheer! A regiment of volunteers was marching briskly towards the Park, their bayonets flashing bright in the sunlight. Was there a reaction? Had the forces of order rallied? Had the progress of the Attila been checked? In a very short time I was in the street, greedy for information. Accosting an officer, I asked him what was the news. He said that the aëronef had ceased dropping petroleum, that a vigorous reaction had taken place, that the conflagrations were partly checked, while the anarchists and rioters were being driven mercilessly from the streets with bullet and cold steel. Without more ado I ran back into the house, and, shouting the good tidings to old Northerton, enlisted him forthwith for an expedition.

Our plan of campaign was speedily agreed upon. We would make our way to Hyde Park, and find out all about the destruction of last night from the crowds who would be sure to gather there.

Mrs. Northerton and Lena protested, as was only to be expected, but very little attention, I am afraid, was paid to them. Taking a satchel of provisions and a couple of flasks of claret with us, we left the ladies to brood over our temerity at their leisure. One thing must be added. Though it seemed improbable that chances would favour me, I stuffed into my breast pocket poor Mrs. Hartmann's last letter. It certainly would not be my fault if her fiendish son failed to get it, and having got it, to relish it.

We followed the regiment for a while till Westbourne Grove was reached. The heat, smoke, and dust here were intolerable, and whole clumps of buildings were still merrily blazing. Every now and then the crack of rifles could be heard, and we knew that somewhere or other justice was being summarily administered. At this point a stranger, evidently a gentleman, stepped up and asked us if we had heard the latest. We answered that both the events of the night and early morning were for the most part unknown to us. Thereupon he stated that all through the night fires were being kindled in every direction by the aëronef. It had been discovered, too, that hundreds, if not thousands, of confederates were pushing on this abominable work below, and that these by inciting the mob to violence had greatly assisted to swell the terrible list of catastrophes. He added that the aëronef had drawn off awhile and was wheeling idly around the Park in wide circles, occasionally discharging her guns whenever the crowds grew dense. Meantime, order had been partially restored – the military, albeit many soldiers were suspected of complicity, had been called out; the police, at first helpless, had rallied; and volunteer regiments and special police corps were pouring on to the different scenes of action. Anarchists and rioters were being shot down in batches, and it was believed that all co-operation with the aëronef from below had been at last practically extirpated. Then came an announcement which moved me to barely repressed excitement. The aëronef during the early morning had been seen to descend in the Park and to deposit four men, subsequently rising to her old altitude. The police were now searching for them in all directions, and it was said that their arrest was imminent.

"Did you hear of the balloon attack?" continued our communicative informant.

"No," we replied in unison, deeply interested.

"Well, some time after midnight, the thought occurred to Bates, the aëronaut, that this aëronef might possibly be fought in her own element. In the grounds of the Military Exhibition in South Kensington was the balloon used for visitors' ascents. Providing himself with a rifle and three well-charged bombs – a terribly risky thing no doubt, but look at the emergency! – he had the silk inflated, and, the wind suiting, rose up steadily, meaning to get above his opponent, and, if possible, shatter her with his missiles. Unfortunately the blaze rushing up from a newly-fired group of mansions revealed the daring aëronaut. It was a pretty, if a terrible picture – the little balloon drifting up towards the mighty aëronef in the glow of those blazing roofs."

"Did he get near enough to throw?"

"No, poor fellow. A journalist who was below with a night-glass says that he never had even a chance. One of the men on the deck of the aëronef pulled out a revolver and fired, and the balloon, pierced through and through, at once began to descend rapidly. On its reaching the ground with a shock in Earl's Court Road, the bombs exploded, and the car and its plucky occupant were shattered to pieces."

"Poor chap. A wild attempt, but rats in a hole cannot be particular," said old Northerton.

Thanking our informant heartily we moved hastily on, both eager to see something of the movements of the terrible vessel.

The landing of the four men did not perplex me for long; Schwartz, as I knew, had been prepared to descend. But why four in this enterprise for which one alone had been originally picked?

The solution which suggested itself to me was this. Despite the devastation he had caused, Hartmann was very dissatisfied with the result. His vast outlay of material had not effected the ruin of one-fifth part of the great city, while in all probability the resources of the Attila were becoming somewhat strained. Relative to her size these resources were undoubtedly slender, and it was requisite, accordingly, to devise some new and less costly mode of attack. Of the lull in the work of the incendiaries Hartmann must have got wind, but not knowing the cause of it, and anxious to secure a redoubled activity below – now so indispensable to his success – he had despatched four of the crew to fan their energies into fury. That their efforts would be futile was now certain enough; the problematical part of the affair was the supposition that they would ever get back to their baffled leader at all. Probably they were now bitterly regretting their temerity, if, indeed, they had not been shot against the wall by the furious restorers of order.

Just then a squad of soldiers passed by escorting some incendiaries, whose faces filthy with grime and brutal to a degree filled us with loathing and anger.

They were to be shot in a neighbouring mews, and, if the accounts we heard were reliable, richly deserved their fate. What kicks their captors were giving them! The faces seemed unfamiliar to me, all alike of a low grade of ruffianism such as every great city breeds, but which never declares its strength till the day of weakness arrives. But suddenly one of the wretches, who lagged somewhat behind the rest, received a sharp cuff from a soldier, and in the volley of curses that followed I recognized a well-known and long-detested voice. It was that of Michael Schwartz, who, bruised, handcuffed, befouled with grime and dirt, was being driven like a bullock to a slaughter-house. How savage a despair must have goaded him in the last few minutes of his dark and damnable life! I turned away with a shudder, glad however to think that this fiend at least was no longer to cumber the ground. Might the three other men of his party meet with the same luck!

After half-an-hour's walk we found ourselves in Hyde Park. Our informant had not misled us. High above the sward circled the Attila, her graceful flight and vast bulk, her silvery-grey sides and projecting aëroplane, her long ruddy flag streaming over the screw-blades, her ram-like horned bow, and above all, her now hideous repute, rendering her a weirdly conspicuous object.

Old Mr. Northerton's face was a picture; the look he bent on me was one of unconcealed and almost childish wonder at the aëronef and of deep respect for his would-be son-in-law, who had actually trodden its deck. He seemed fascinated by the wondrous air vessel, and lamented loudly that its conception should have lodged in so unworthy and fiendish a mind.

"Think what a good man might have effected for his kind, for their creature-comforts and commerce, for the cause of civilization, science, and culture. A fleet of such ships would render England monarch of the nations and arm her with power to sweep away hordes of monstrous iniquities. War could be finally stamped out, and universal arbitration substituted for it."

"Until France or Russia began to launch similar fleets," I added, for it seemed clear enough that nations who could fight with armies and ironclads would have no insuperable prejudice against fighting with airships. If only one nation possessed these aëronefs she would, doubtless, silence the rest, but in actual practice inventions of this character cannot be permanently kept secret.

There were very few persons in the Park, for the dread of the aëronef was universal. Her guns dexterously singled out crowds, hence no one wished to recruit them, and any symptom of their formation in the neighbourhood speedily corrected itself.

Outside the railings, indeed, there were plenty of onlookers, but there the military patrolled the streets, and bodies of mounted police vigorously seconded their efforts. I was told by a bystander that severe fighting was going on in East London, but that nothing serious of late was reported from the West End. This sounded all very well, but what if the Attila was once more to re-open fire? How about the restoration of order then? Would regiments clear the streets under bomb fire? Would police hunt down incendiaries in the teeth of petroleum showers? The man admitted that in that case chaos must follow, but, nevertheless, he reckoned the vessel was emptied.

"She can't hold much more stuff at any rate."

The reed was unfortunately slender, as he had shortly cause to discover.

I was gazing at the stray onlookers around us when a strange group caught my eye. Two men had just entered the Park, followed by a third, with his hat pulled well forward over his brow. The two men in advance were talking excitedly, and pointed at intervals to the aëronef. Something in their faces riveted my attention, and, as they came nearer, I recognized Norris among them, ay, and the villainous Thomas himself was bringing up the rear. What were they doing here at such an hour? My notion was that their mission had completely failed, that their associates were being shot down, and that they were now seeking a haven from danger in the Attila. But was it possible that they could be embarked in the broad light of day in the face of crowd, police, and military? Were they even expected back so early from the fulfilment of their task? Whatever the explanation might be – one thing was clear, the chance for my letter had come! As Norris passed me I looked him full in the face – he grew pale as death, and I saw him feel spasmodically for his revolver. Evidently he thought that I should denounce him, and was prepared to die biting. Of course no semblance of such a plan had crossed my mind. Hateful to me as were these anarchists, they had treated me well on the Attila, and with them I had once amicably broken salt. Honour shielded even the enemies of the human race from such a scurvy return.

Brushing past Norris I whispered: "A letter – for the captain," stuffing it dexterously into his hand at the same time. This action passed wholly unnoticed even by Norris' companions, while the worthy ex-Commissioner was far too well absorbed in the aëronef to mark my brief departure from his side. Norris himself passed on hurriedly, directing his steps to the central portion of the Park. I watched the three anarchists till they reached an almost deserted spot, about four hundred yards off, and it then became evident that they were bent on signalling to the Attila. For aught I knew Hartmann in his conning-tower was even now sweeping the sward with his powerful field-glass.

I saw Norris produce something out of the breast of his coat, and fuddle eagerly about it with his companions. The anarchists then lay down on the grass, and seemed to be awaiting some answer. It was some time, however, before I seized the true rendering of their conduct, and but for a stray yellow gleam showing up between Norris and one of the others I should not have seized it at all. The device adopted was simple. The gallant three were evidently being waited and watched for. To ensure notice they had agreed to exhibit a large yellow flag, and for security's sake they had unrolled this at full length on the grass, lying round it at the same time so as to screen it from observation. The problem remaining was, how the Attila would get them safely on board. She was, perhaps, two hundred and fifty feet above them at the moment, and the difficulty in such a situation seemed almost insuperable.

Suddenly a cry from Mr. Northerton arrested me. The aëronef was curving swiftly in and out, so as to trace a sort of descending spiral. Then when nearly over the flag she stopped almost dead, and seemed to be falling rapidly.

"It's falling! it's falling!" yelled Mr. Northerton.

But I knew better, that fall was adjusted by the sand-levers.

The Attila sank slowly to the ground. The police, military, and spectators outside and inside the railing rushed forward to the scene with loud cries of exultation. All were seized with the desire to be in at the death, to vent their rage on the foe who now seemed to have lost his might. It was with the greatest trouble that I held Mr. Northerton back. He was carried away by the sight of the thousands streaming into the Park, and converting in masses on the fallen monster. They were now close up. Several rifle-cracks told that the soldiers to the fore were already hotly engaged, were perhaps striving to storm the hull.

And then came a dread disenchantment.

16. The Last of the Attila

As the rabble closed on the aëronef, she gave a huge heave, her bow swinging over her assailants like the tilted arm of a see-saw. Next, the stern cleared the turf and the colossus rose majestically, rolling the while like some ship riding at anchor. The gnats who clung to her bottom and gallery dropped off confusedly, and the whole multitude in her neighbourhood seemed bewildered with surprise and terror. Suddenly the Attila was enveloped in flame and smoke; the roar of her big pieces mingling with the cracks of the machine-guns and the rifle fire that spurted from the loop-holes in her armour. Lanes were cut in the crowd in all directions, and a veritable hail of bullets whistled past the spot where we stood, many even claiming their victims around us. Discretion, not valour, was our choice. We made wildly for the outlets toward which a screaming mob rushed behind us, and, once through them, made our way rapidly down the street.

Having run some few hundred yards we stopped, and saw with dismay how narrow had been our escape. The Attila was still rising majestically with her machine and quick-firing guns playing on the multitude as a hose plays on flames. The wretched victims were fighting for the blocked gates and outlets like creatures possessed, bloody gaps opened and shut in their midst, and heaps of butchered and trampled bodies tripped up the frantic survivors in batches as they ran. The din was simply unearthly; the picture as a whole indescribable, not being set off by two or three easily detachable features, but so compositely appalling in its details as to baffle the deftest pen. It lingers still vividly in my memory. The cloudy pall above, the still smoking and ruined houses opposite the Park, the heaving crowd with its multitudinous detail of slaughter, suffocation, and writhings, the smoke-clad hull of the Attila, as it rose in angry majesty, its top peering like the Matterhorn through clouds – these were fraught with a fascination that held us enthralled. The sight would have moved the pity of a Borgia, and glutted to the full the morbid æstheticism of a Nero.

But the massacre was as short as it was swift. When the aëronef had reached the height of one hundred and fifty feet she suddenly ceased firing, and began once more to circle with albatross-like grace in the path she had previously favoured.

What was the motive for this strange suspension of hostilities? Possibly her munitions were failing, and the thought of departure with his grim project unaccomplished had forced Hartmann to husband his resources and await some novel opportunities for mischief at night. His state of mind, however, must have been even at that moment unenviable. That he had yet received the fatal letter might, or might not, be the case. But quite apart from this thunderbolt, he had a gloomy prospect to brood over. The failure of his artillery and petroleum to effect the ruin he had contemplated was in itself – from his standpoint – a catastrophe, while the extirpation of the anarchist rising below rendered his very security dubious. Of the success or defeat of the Continental anarchists we had as yet heard nothing, owing to the disorganization of the usual channels of information, but, seeing that the attack in London had failed, it was highly probable that it had withered away utterly in places where there was no Attila to back it. In this event the situation of Hartmann would be precarious. Defiant of human effort as seemed the aëronef, it was, nevertheless, to a large extent dependent on the maintenance of its communication with society – communications which had hitherto been kept up with the various Continental anarchist groups. Coals, provisions, gas, munitions of all sorts had to be allowed for. But in the débâcle of modern anarchism and complete exposure of its secrets, things might come to such a pass that the Attila would be altogether without a basis, deprived of which her death from starvation was a mere question of time. Here was a fine opportunity for the Governments, an opportunity which could not well have escaped the acute vision of Hartmann. Ah, well, we should see.

At this stage my speculations were cut short by a rush of fugitives down the street, and, unable to breast the torrent, we took the wisest course and flowed with it. Some way further on, however, the panic began to ease down, then slowly died away, until many stopped outright to gaze on the destroyer which sailed so contemptuously above them. Some even found their way back to the Park, anxious to do what they could for the hundreds of wounded and dying wretches who littered the sward for an area of at least three hundred square yards, and whose cries would have shocked the denizens of 'Malebolge'.

We were about to do the same when the road was summarily cleared by police, and all further access to the scene prohibited. We were protesting against this usage when a voice was heard – apparently from one of the rooms of one of the few uninjured houses opposite.

"Hi! here, is that you, Northerton? Come in, man, come in." I looked up and saw leaning from a window an elderly gentleman whom I recognized as a frequent visitor at Carshalton Terrace. We accepted forthwith this very seasonable invitation, and mounting the steps, were ushered into a cosy drawing-room where we found the whole family assembled.

The old gentleman, whose name was Wingate, could talk of nothing, of course, but the one absorbing subject, the Attila and her depredations. An attentive circle surrounded us as we recounted the story of the last shameful massacre.

"The ship, or whatever you call it, seems quiet again," observed our host.

"A calm before a storm I am afraid; I dread to think what this night may have in store for us."

"And I too. My idea of the respite is simply this – they are waiting till darkness comes on, and will take merciless advantage of the facilities it offers for the creation of panics and confusion."

"I hear," continued Mr. Wingate, "that the fires are being got under control, but that Westminster, Southwark, Brompton, Kensington, the City, and adjoining districts are no better than smoking ruins! Heaven shield us from this monster!"

"By the way," I put in, "have you a good spyglass here? There goes the destroyer almost within hail."

"Yes; there's a capital one upstairs which used to do duty at sea when I was a yachtsman."

I followed him out of the room, leaving my future father-in-law with the ladies.

Mr. Wingate took me into the bedroom immediately above, and drawing a leather case from the shelf produced a capital instrument. He had a long look first, but complained of the difficulty of following the movements of the aëronef. He then handed it to me to report, if possible, better results. Lifting the window I lay back on the floor against the side of the bed, and, steadying the barrel on the edge of the dressing-table, managed to obtain an excellent view.

"Do you see anything?"

"Yes, she's turning our way. Ah! that's better. How delicate this glass is!"

I then described to him the prominent parts of the Attila more or less in detail.

"Is the deck crowded?"

"No; there are several men round the battery near the citadel, but the rest of the deck is deserted. Here, try again. The view now is splendid."

The glass once more changed hands.

"What a sight!" ejaculated my companion, having succeeded in 'spotting' the aëronef. "Why, I can see the whole thing just as if it was only across the road. Just as you described it, too. By the way, there is a solitary individual pacing the fore-deck frantically. He seems terribly excited about something.

More mischief doubtless."

"Describe him!" I cried eagerly.

"Easier said than done," he said. "A moment ago the whole thing was as clear as if it was only across the road. He seems very tall, rather dark, with a thick, black beard, and he holds some letter in his hand, which he kisses and then brandishes fiercely."

"Hartmann, by all that's holy!" Vindictively I bethought me of the letter, and the miserable reports of failure which Norris and his men must have delivered.

"I should say he is the captain or some other boss in authority, for, see, a gunner comes up and salutes him. Ha, he must be angry! He dismisses the man fiercely, and seems once more to devour the letter."

"Go on, go on!"

"He steps to the railing and shakes his fist at the City below. Now he seems to be deliberating, for he remains perfectly still, looking every now and then at the letter or document. How beside himself with anger he seems! He dashes his fist on the railing, now he strides across the deck and stalks through the surprised gunners to the citadel. I feel sure something terrible is brewing."

Ha, captain of the Attila! Smart under the lash of Nemesis! Matricide and murderer, writhe! You felt not for the thousands sacrificed for a theory; feel now for the report of your plans wrecked beyond hope of repair.

Feel, too, for a loved mother, the sole creature you ever cared for, but whom your reckless and futile savagery has immolated! Hater of your race, terrible indeed has been your penalty!

"Hallo! He comes up again with a revolver in each hand. He closes the gate of the outer wall of the citadel, and seems to harangue the crew. Is he mad or what? He fires one of the revolvers, and a man drops. A mutiny! a mutiny! I see the men rushing up like fanatics. They climb the wall, he shooting the while. Ha! he rushes into the citadel, and closes the inner door sharply. They try to follow him, but cannot!" After a long pause – "Stay, they have broken the door open, and rush..."

A flash that beggared the Levin-bolt, a crash shattering the window-panes and deadening the ear, a shock hurling us both on our backs, broke the utterance. Then thundered down a shower of massive fragments, fragments of the vast ship whose decks I had once trodden. Hartmann, dismayed with the failure of his plans and rendered desperate by the letter, had blown up the Attila! The news of his failure and the message of a dying woman had done what human hatred was too impotent even to hope for.

But little more remains to be said. You are conversant with the story of the next few days. You know also how order was once more completely re-established, how the wreckage of that fell twenty-four hours was slowly replaced by modern buildings, how gradually the Empire recovered from the shock, and how dominant henceforth became the great problems of labour. My own connection with these latter was not destined to endure. After my marriage with Lena, my interests took a different turn. Travel and literary studies left no room for the earlier duties of the demagogue. Writing from this quiet German retreat I can only hope that my brief narrative will prove of some interest to you. It has not been my aim to write history. I have sought to throw light only on one of its more romantic corners, and if I have succeeded in doing so, the whole purpose of my efforts will have been accomplished.

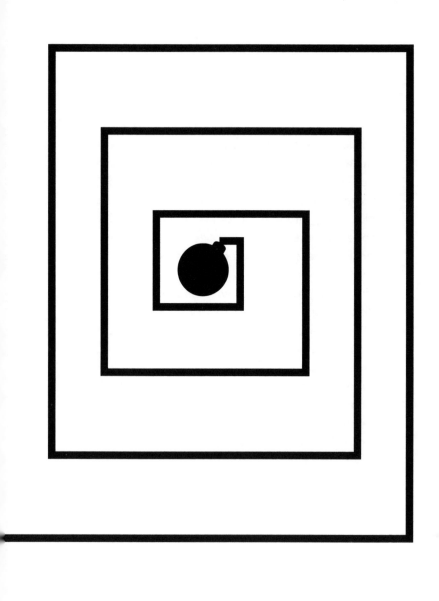

Bone is an imprint of Tangent Books

Ian Bone is the author of Bash the Rich –
available from our website. If you enjoyed this, why not try:

A True Account of the Villainous Bartholomew Rakehell – ne'er do well
by Nicholas Law

An epic tale of Bordellos, Boxing and Buccaneers

*"Genius… extraordinary, brilliantly observed,
uproarious and touching."*

Where's My Money?
by Mike Manson

Life in a dole office during the endless summer of '76

*"Full of brilliantly observed characters, consistently witty
and carries a poignant punch."*

Unsettled: In a Hole, Climbed a Mountain
by Graham Walker

Stories of life on the streets and selling the Big Issue

*"Every house should have one – including
the House of Commons and the Lords."*

www.tangentbooks.co.uk